36/24   £5
Ac

Louise Stanley lives in Hampshire, England. She has been writing stories set in the Insulan Empire since reading *Germinal* by Emile Zola and *Crime and Punishment* by Fyodor Dostoyevsky as a teenager and thinking how cool it would be if those books had magic in them.

To David and Susan, and Tony and Ann. Thanks to the mods and posters on RPG.net, /r/fantasywriters and /r/worldbuilding

www.louise-stanley.co.uk
www.facebook.com/ninelivesofmichalpiech

TALES FROM THE INSULAN EMPIRE

LOUISE STANLEY

Includes preview chapters for the upcoming novellas "Thin Ice" and "Deep Water"

Preface: Close Encounters of the Magical Kind

from How Sorcery Came About, *a preface from* A Child's Treasury of Magical Tales, *published by Bauer u. Sohn Verlag, Galistow, 1,978 IC, in Breston translation.*

When the gods created the world, it floated in a sea of magic. There was no barrier between the heavens and Orbis, and as a result, everything was so chaotic that the rhythm of life was constantly interrupted. In order for the laws of nature to keep working, and for the world to retain its shape, there had to be a curtain separating orderly nature from the disorderly cosmos.

Fricka and Minerva therefore took it upon themselves to create this curtain – Fricka spun the thread which Minerva wove into cloth. Eventually, their vast tapestry was strung across the heavens. They dyed it blue in honour of Odin, to complement the grass and trees which Lisak had decided should be green, and thus created the daytime sky. It was thin enough that the sun and moon could still be seen through it, but thick enough to keep magic from affecting the mechanisms that the gods had already set in motion and had no desire to see disrupted. All was well: life evolved and spread out over the planet, confident that it would be left in peace for the gods to enjoy their handiwork. The first humans made their homes in caves and gradually constructed homes of wood and stone, ploughing and sowing, taming the creatures that shared Orbis, and spreading across the world, beyond the seas – north, south, east and west.

But the Devil, Perkonus, was annoyed. Magic was his creation, and he thrived on the uncertainty it had originally introduced into creation. He wasn't strong enough to rip the curtain down, because the gods of the Family held it too tightly, and one is not enough to overcome four. So instead, he took a needle, and poked holes in it, in all sorts of random places – these became the stars.

Through the holes leaked magic. Spirits found a way of communicating with the mortal world. The same magic which allowed the dead to speak to the living allowed beliefs and fears to become reality, objects to defy the laws of gravity and momentum, and people to change their appearances and shapes. A great cathedral or mosque may appear bigger on the inside than it is on the outside, in testament to the earnest reverence of those who build it, but roads and rivers may change course on the whim of imps to confuse travellers. Spirits of the recent dead may give comfort to their loved ones, but some unfortunate souls may be trapped between worlds if the Devil is allowed to interfere too much – and people let him into their hearts more often than is good for them. Magic was never powerful enough to twist nature out of shape, but it must be considered as the source of a great many interesting – and troubling – things.

The gods saw that this had been done, and could not undo it. Rather, they taught people how to use magic carefully, and granted their favour to wise individuals who were tasked with stewarding this power. They allowed the secrets of healing to be sown amongst the peoples of the world, and provided shamans with spoken guidance and wisdom when needed. Humanity has not always husbanded sorcery as we should, but faith in a divine plan comforts the just and tries to counteract the wicked.

Like a knife might be used to cut bread or wound someone, so magic may be used for good or evil. It is, however, always erratic and dangerous. It must be treated with respect – as many find out through their own experimentation.

These stories show how people encounter magic, and what they do with it.

Contents

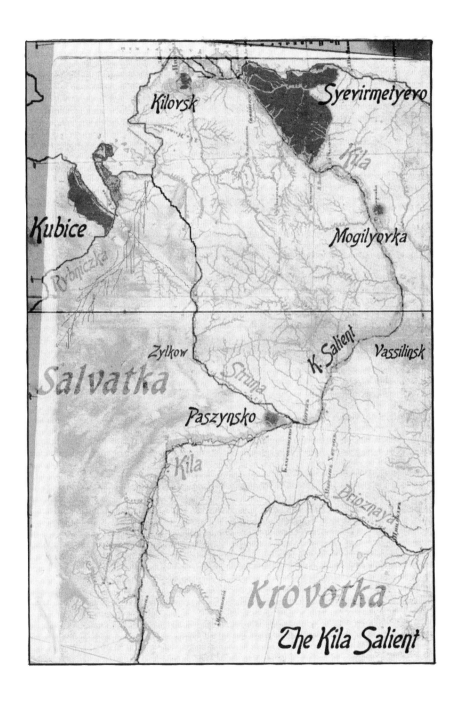

Kilovsk

Syevirmetyevo

Kila

Kubice

Mogilyovka

Rybniczka

Zylkow

K. Salient

Vassilinsk

Salvatka

Struna

Paszynsko

Kila

Drioznaya

Krovotka

The Kila Salient

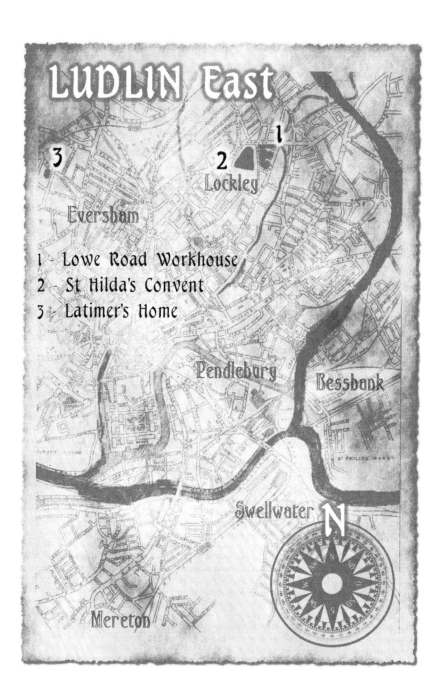

LUDLIN East

3

2 ◣◰ 1

Lockley

Eversham

1 - Lowe Road Workhouse
2 - St Hilda's Convent
3 - Latimer's Home

Pendlebury

Bessbank

Swellwater

N

Mereton

THE CAT'S TAIL

The Cat's Tail

"Clear off, Pussy-Willow," came his brother's voice from behind him in the front passage between the back parlour and the shop-front.

Simon Seymour jumped out of the way as if Patrick had set his trousers on fire.

"No-one can get through with your arse in the way." Patrick gave his brother a playful shove further out towards the door. "Go and get us some liquorice." The demand was followed up with a shield coin shoved into his palm.

When someone gives you a coin, you have to obey them; that was what his father said. "Ten groschen worth?" Simon asked his brother.

"Yeah, why not? It'll keep us going for a few days. Don't eat any on the way home."

Simon turned the coin over in his hands. He normally only got to handle coppers – a groschen for a piece of liquorice or a sweet roll or two for a glass of lemonade or a large sugar mouse. Patrick had his own jar of coins which he was supposed to share with him, but he decided what they bought with them. When Simon was nine, his ma said, he'd get to have his own jar and spend his money just how he pleased. Until then, Patrick was the one who had a coin jar and chose what they bought. "You're neither beggars nor gentlefolk," was what Pa always told them at tea. "It's up to me to teach you how to work for your living."

At the church school there were children who went home to the huts on the sand. Pa always told him to be thankful they had a real house. As Simon went past the door into the shop, Pa was standing there now. "Don't step in any puddles!" he said, patting his son on the head and shoulder from inside the shop itself. Not that he was going to anyway, but just in case. "When you come back you can fold some of the cloth for me and wipe the counters."

Outside, the sun glinted off the damp cobbles and the gold lettering of the sign above the front windows. The blustery winter weather in the coastal town of Tidemarsh meant that every spring, Pa had to spend a Restday sprucing up the sign. He himself would do most of the painting, but Patrick, who would announce to all and sundry he was now *nine*, was helping apply the dark green background. Then Pa could delicately apply the gilding to the letters: ALEXANDER SEYMOUR AND SONS – DRAPERY AND CLOTH MERCHANT. It had just been re-done, and Simon's chest swelled with pride as he looked up at it. Now he had his letters, it made more sense; he stopped to read it every time he came in and out, marvelling that the elegant pattern could have become the sounds he'd heard every day indoors before that. Everything he could get his hands on with letters on it, he read until over and over it made sense to him, although even Patrick still had to ask Pa what some words meant.

After reading it once, Simon turned down the road to the beach; the sweet-shop was on the seafront near the fishing harbour. He might watch the ships for a bit, but he'd need to get back before his brother was sent to look for him. He carefully skirted the puddles, sensibly not dipping the toe of his shoes into the murky water…

"Hey, boy!"

As Simon reached the end of the road and was about to turn the corner towards the promenade, a tall man wearing whiskers and a fur collar had hailed him. He was about the age of Simon's grandpa, who had owned the shop before Pa and now lived in the cottage beside them and helped Pa with his "books" – huge ledgers full of letters and numbers which Patrick knew were the business records, because Pa knew all about cloth but had always found numbers awkward. Simon looked up into bespectacled eyes, but the gentleman pointed down at his shoes and handed him a handkerchief. "Would you be so kind as to clean them?"

Clean his *shoes*? At home they had a maid to do that, a girl from the docks who said she had worked for his mother's family. "Our Harriet might do it for you, sir."

"I'll give you a half-shield, then," the man said, his lip curling in what Simon took to be disgust. The boy felt a shiver down his spine, like he did when Patrick found him with his hand inside the coin jar and he had yet to turn round to see his brother standing there ready to twist his ears off. "I'm sure your mamma and papa would be grateful for that – if they're still alive."

"My pa works for his living," Simon said, puffing out his chest.

"I suppose he must," the gentleman replied with an exasperated sigh, "but small boys usually need to learn a trade too."

"I'm going to be a soldier when I grow up," Simon protested. "But I can't go to the army until I'm sixteen. I have someone to clean my shoes. Don't you have anyone to do it for you?"

The old man opened his mouth to speak, but no words came out for a whole minute. "Well, I never…!" he eventually managed to splutter. "Such impudence from one so young! And after I offered something in return, that might be valued by someone who chances to be on the streets at this hour of the morning."

"It's a holiday," Simon said. "Saint Something-or-Other. I think it's a She." He struggled to recall exactly why they got this particular day off school, but the churches closed so the priests could pray, and everyone else carried on as normal, except they might have slices of hot roast beef for tea and Pa, Ma and Grandpa might have a glass of wine. They all went to church on Restsday like everyone else, but only after they'd painted the shop.

Or something like that. It all ran together in his mind, probably because he was angry and he felt the crackling and burning in his fingers, because the old man was being quite *rude*. And if there was one thing Pa had told him not to be, it was *rude*.

"Saint *Helena*," the gentleman corrected him, crossing himself with the points of the compass like his mother did when she was scared. "In my day," the man went on, "there was proper respect for the gods and for respectable people…People were more grateful…Boy, are you listening to me?"

"But I *am* grateful," Simon protested, swallowing his anger even though it hurt him. "Look! My brother gave me a whole shield from his coin jar just to buy liquorice. A half-shield might buy a few sugar mice..."

"Then it won't trouble you to do it for me," came the gentleman's reply. "You could have your mice and your liquorice all at once."

He didn't want to tell the man to *go away*, but he wished very hard that he would. The man's voice appeared to resonate inside his mind – that he still didn't believe him about his family, and was just playing along so Simon would do his bidding like a good peasant should. It was an odd sensation, but he'd noticed it before – like the reflection of a face in a mirror, but instead of a true reflection of someone's image, it told him what they really wanted to say but couldn't.

He hadn't taken the old man's coin, so he didn't have to clean his shoes. If he had, he'd have been obliged to do it there and then; when his Pa was in a good mood, he often gave him a groschen to cut the cloth, and he'd do it. He also refused to lower himself to doing what the maid did for them. He liked Harriet, but she had her place in the household, helping Ma in the kitchen and the laundry and cleaning the shop in the evening. She ate with them at their table and slept in the spare room in Grandpa's cottage.

"*No*," he repeated. He fixed the man in the eyes. Pa had told him not to do that, not to mirror the gazes of gentlefolk, because even though he had nothing to be ashamed of as a Seymour, it was best not to "rock the boat". But he now did so defiantly, as if he were a cockatrice trying to turn the man to stone.

Now that *would* be fun. The next time Patrick boxed his ears, he'd be able to get his own back.

But anyway, if the gentleman was going to be so wicked, he would be wicked back. "I'm not a peasant. Even if I was, I wouldn't clean your shoes!"

The old man recoiled from him as if he'd shown him an amulet like the priests wore. Grandpa had once complained of a knocking noise at night in his room, things moved all over the place and a draft on the stairs in the middle of summer. Mother Jones, who always took the services and gave communion, had come from the church with her holy charm. Grandpa had been less uncomfortable after that, and indeed his cottage had been a little warmer and lighter afterwards. Now the man looked about him.

There were heavy footsteps on the paving stones behind them. "Simon? What the Perkins is going on here?"

It was Pa. He was so angry he wasn't avoiding any of the puddles. He came up to the crotchety old twig of a gentleman and the old man melted away.

"There was a *mistake* here, sir. I do apologise – I had no idea..."

"No-one insults my sons," Pa said. "If you leave now, I'll lay no hand on you." Simon had often seen Pa do this to customers who tried to swindle him or people hanging about the door of the shop without coming in or going away of their own will. The old man slunk off, his hands with nothing else to do but claw the air after he put the coin back in his pocket and paddled through the puddles in the road, which would no doubt cause his maid more trouble at home.

Just for fun, I'm going to try something, he thought. *Mother Jones wouldn't like it, and I'm sure she'll be helping him when he finds out what's happened, but she doesn't have to know it was me.*

He visualised the family's cat, the real Pussy Willow, a ragged old tabby Pa was always throwing things at when he thought Ma wasn't looking. He saw her tail arched in the air behind her as she sauntered along the wall next to their outhouse. He also saw the tail attached to the old man's backside in his mind's eye. His fingers itched.

"Go on, Simon, run off to the shop and get your sweets," Pa said, with another slap on his back. "Don't linger – there and back, please."

Simon slipped away down the street, looking back one last time as he followed the gentleman down to the promenade. He saw the results of his charm-casting: a long, grey-and-white tail curling up into the air, larger than Willow's and comfortably sized for his scissors-skinny frame.

He smiled.

He mustn't do this too much, but it felt good to be able to get his own back. Small boys had trades too – and being a *magician* was definitely a fine line of work to be in.

Recueil des Édits,

§. XIV.

THE DOCTRINE OF THE IMPENETRABILITY OF MAGICAL EVIDENCE

SOMMAIRE.

L E *serus... au fond d'autrui, sans captiver* *des maitres de fossés.* *Village, ne* *aucun cens* *le ord du Seigneur.* *Ibidem.*

toutes matieres de mines soient houilles, charbons & autres, és Cité, franchise, banlieu & pays de Liege, sçavoir faisons à tous & un chacun qu'il appartiendra, qu'étants requis de la part Noble Seigr. Jean Merode Seigr de Viller &c. de donner attestation de la verité sur le fait des usages, observances & coûtumes de charbonages, à Nous verbalement remontre de sa part, apres avoir consulté ensemble, & avite nos registres & usages, Avons certifié & attesté, certifions & attestons, que personne de quel état, qualité ou condition il soit, ne peut entrer, loŭoyes, ouvrir n'abstraire mines de houilles & charbons, ny prendre paires, voies & commodites, en fu & bien, heritage & fond d'autruy, & qu'il ederoit comme luy appartenant, sans le pré & consentement ... proprie ... peine ... cherché & ... peines & condemnation, suivant les ... usages, & de ne point ... ulterieurement, ne soit qu'il y ... ou ... même au ... Seigneur ... ou Seigneurie ... ne ... de ... ny ... droit ... terre ... pour cause du bien ... quelque ... superficiel ... posséde par le chai ... Nous les voir ... Werlea, Gille Crosier, & Jacque ... ier ou son Subd ... la Saint...

§. X ... du charbon ... O ...

M ... cens ... discontinu ...

... franchise & Banlieu du Pays ... appartiendra, que cu ... & u ... chai ... devant nous comparu hon ... personnellement ... faisant tant pour eux

The Doctrine of the Impenetrability of Magical Evidence

An extract from the Rechtsprinzip, *the main Insulan Empire legal textbook, published Thorry (1st Month) 1,983 IC, written by Justice W Hale of the Ludlin Central Municipal Courts.*

1● Society has historically wrestled with the problem of how to arbitrate cases predicated on the willful use of magic (commonly known, and referred to hereafter, as sorcery), either deliberate or involuntary. Prior to the reforms of the Empress Sophia, persecution of sorcery was rife, and the number of people convicted of witchcraft on minimal evidence [1] or extra-judicially murdered was alarming. It is believed to be mainly a by-product of religious sectarianism prior to the War of Settlement, which led to the foundation of the modern State. Those convicted of actual crimes perpetrated by sorcerous means are believed to be many times less numerous than those convicted after malicious denunciation for the material or social gain of an accuser or during periods of religious mania now repudiated by all the faiths of Insula.

2. Empress Sophia laid down in law two significant legal doctrines. Here, The Doctrine of the Impenetrability of Magical Evidence, commonly abbreviated as the *Doctrine of Impenetrability*, protects those who might be arraigned for sorcerous crimes on hearsay evidence, or sorcery itself, while preventing the use of genuine supernatural means to prosecute or condemn any Citizen or Subject [2].

The *Doctrine* is as follows:

a. A crime allegedly committed by sorcerous means cannot be prosecuted without clear, supporting, mundane evidence. Eyewitness testimony must be without prejudice in this matter and must be thoroughly scrutinised by counsel.

b. No magically-derived or divined evidence will be admitted in judicial proceedings. This extends to non-criminal jurisdictions including probate cases. [3]

c. No supernatural being, ghost, spirit, domovoi, djinni etc. may testify in court, file suit, or stand trial for a crime committed against living persons.

d. Sorcery is not a crime absent any other act which would normally be considered criminal when committed by mundane means.

3. This principle applies at all levels of the civilian and military systems of justice, including the manorial system. Ecclesiastical [4] and other professional tribunals are exempt, as are private institutions separate from the State. The *Doctrine* is also in operation in the new colonial Territories in the process of absorption into the Empire, Lenkija and Vesgale [5].

4. Case Studies. Because the militia and local magistrates usually decline to prosecute most vexatious accusations, recent incidences of the *Doctrine* being tested in court are rare. However, they include two of the most politically and socially important cases of recent times.

a. *Ex parte Čaikovskis*, 1,970 IC. The strength of the evidence against Ernest Čaikovskis, the Vesgali spy, was enough to send him to the gallows without the wrinkle in his case involving magic. However, on being caught trying to squeeze through the bars of the window in his cell in the form of a gull, the prison governor's actions placing him in solitary confinement on a convicted-persons ward at Long Bank prison for the duration of his period of pre-trial detention were endorsed by the Chief Justice of Brest, Henry Belkin.

b. *Krovotka v Medvedev, 1,981 IC.* Sergei Medvedev was found guilty by reasons of insanity of mauling his children while in bear form. After examination by medical and shamanistic practitioners, Medvedev was judged to have shapechanged while angry, in the middle of the legitimate corporal chastisement of his children. Sorcery held to be unpremeditated is treated the same way as other temporary insanities.

5. This article is of current interest after *Medvedev* as it is clear that the case better defines voluntary and involuntary sorcery. Those with similar familiar spirits [6] are clearly at risk after public outrage at the case, which has the potential to erupt into outright violence against vulnerable individuals should there be another such case. Legal Practitioners are reminded that the Diet has continuously rejected calls for the repudiation of the *Doctrine*. Egregious convictions have not come to light in the manorial or urban magistrates' courts, even for summary offences or other mischief. However, extra care must be taken when handling accusations of such "crimes", as the rule of law has always been a thin veneer over popular anarchy.

William Hale, Justice, Widder (9th Month), 1,982 IC.

Endnotes

[1] A common penalty for sorcerous crimes was burning at the stake. Capital punishment was in greater use prior to the reforms of the

XXth century IC, but this punishment was noted even by contemporary scholars as barbaric and unjust. Empress Sophia was a jurist in her own right, and contributed an essay to the early editions of the *Rechtsprinzip* to this effect, paving the way for her post-War reforms.

[2] A Citizen is a free individual subject to the municipal courts. A Subject is a vassal of a landowner, subject to the manorial courts, an enlisted soldier subject to military courts, or a person otherwise deprived of liberty. Territorial nationals of Lenkija and Vesgale are currently considered Subjects, a status persisting during the process of full absorption into the Empire, whereupon they will gain full status as Citizens. See also The Rights and Duties of the Landowning Classes elsewhere in this volume.

[3] It is this element of the *Doctrine* which gives it its name, despite being judged by scholars to be a trivial clause.

[4] Corporal punishment and writs of excommunication are enacted against clergy accused of "witchcraft". Clear-cut cases include *Synod of Krovt v Modestov*. A manorial case mentioned in the most recent audit of the Gryczewski estate's magistracy, *Graf Gryczewski v Berzina*, was held to be not a flogging for "witchcraft" *per se*, but the case of a priest convicted for other misdemeanours during a riot (assault on a constable and public indecency) in place of conviction by the Krovt Synod for witchcraft, which would have ended her career.

[5] It should be noted that the Vesgali state has hitherto been more discriminatory against alleged sorcerers than its neighbour, largely due to Minervan religious doctrine.

[6] Known variously as *totems, fylgja, rodnidze*, etc.

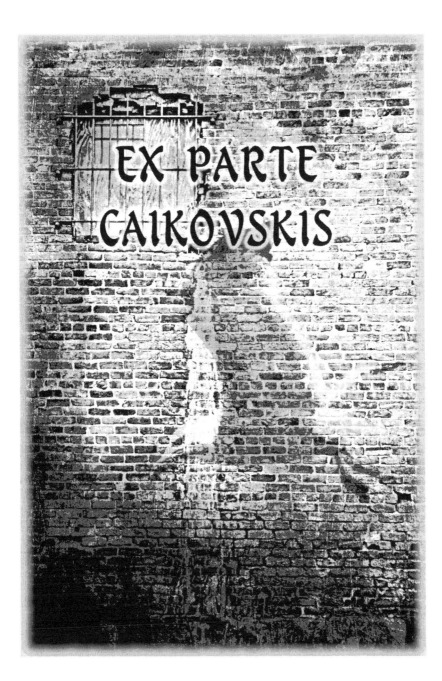

EX PARTE
CAIKOVSKIS

Ex Parte Čaikovskis

BELKIN, H, CHIEF JUSTICE, PROVINCE OF BREST; RAVENSTHORPE HIGH COURT:

Ernest Čaikovskis, was apprehended on 11 Hewn (7th month) 1,970 IC on charges of espionage relating to State documents that found their way into the possession of journalists. Čaikovskis was arraigned for trial in the autumn after the vacation and was held in the remand wing at Long Bank prison, Ludlin, pending the hearing.

However, an incident occurred as follows on 12 Arran (8th month). A warder, John Abbott, served Čaikovskis with his evening meal in his cell, as is the normal arrangement. Abbott was surprised to see the hitherto-locked cell was empty of its detainee. He raised the alarm, but having done so, noticed a bird had become trapped between the bars and the window-glass, open in order to air the cell during the summer months. The animal was observed to be a silver gull (*Larus argentatus*) and in considerable distress.

When additional guards entered the room and released the bird from the grille in which it had become stuck, it became apparent that this was Čaikovskis himself, possessed of a familiar spirit allowing sorcerous changes to his being, as he resumed human form when dislodged. Even though he is of Vesgali minority origin, Čaikovskis' surname is derived from the Slovian word *chaika*, meaning variously lapwing (Salvat) or gull (Krovot).

Accordingly, this judgement is being written in support of the governor's subsequent actions, namely in confining Čaikovskis to a solitary punishment cell in the convicts' wing of the prison. Objections have been raised by counsel as per the Doctrine of the Impenetrability of Magical Evidence (*Rechtsprinzip*, 1,970 IC, 28-31) that this is persecutory of Čaikovskis' rights as a "magician".

Counsel asserts that Čaikovskis was simply exercising his familiar spirit and seeking fresh air on what was a very hot evening, and thus the case falls under the Doctrine's prohibition.

The Doctrine might certainly protect Čaikovskis against arraignment for witchcraft absent any other criminal act. Case law (e.g. *Province of Galtargh versus Grishina, 1/VI/5238 1964 IC*) also prevents successful prosecution of cases predicated on accusations of the manipulation of another person by telepathic or mesmeric means. However, my verdict is that this Doctrine does not apply in this case. Čaikovskis was in the process of committing a crime, in this case attempting to escape from judicially-ordered confinement.

Regarding the explanations offered of his actions, even if Čaikovskis had been wishing to take the air, the window opened onto an unsecured compound – the prison entrance yard – and the wings of a gull permit easy flight. No netting encloses the courtyard below, normally accessible only to free labourers and prison officers and staff. Simply by being in this courtyard, Čaikovskis would have been committing a criminal act, prisoners being afforded the right to exercise at specific times in a secure place, and he had availed himself of these privileges several hours beforehand.

I have no option other than to find in favour of the prison governor.

Objections by counsel dismissed.

BIRTHDATES

Birthdates

"Can't let them get away with it, the murderous bastards."

"What by Pierun the fleet was doing sailing away from Velikoryb at the time I don't know."

"Why you here then?"

"Well…s'appened now, ain't it?"

"They're evacuating Achava. Why aren't they shipping us off? We're closer than they are…"

"They'd 'ave to cross the Middle Mountains to get to us. They'd go for the Salvats first – the road's wide open and Podhalensko's just a coal-heap. Pile of slag's not going to stop 'em if they've already got two cities of ours."

Zbych Piech passed through the outer office on his way into the receiving room. The first posters had gone up yesterday, the ink still wet from the printers; the first advertisements had been placed in the newspapers that day. The first refugees were arriving in Krovt, soaked to the bone with autumn rain.

And the first people were grousing about the Empire's stupidity in moving that damn fleet back to Glasberg, even as they had come to volunteer to defend it.

As the clock struck nine hours, he was greeted by the press of bodies, and a queue that snaked all the way round the side of the Military Hospital in Krovt, several deep. Nothing like the thought that they were only a hundred and fifty versts away from the front to mobilise a city's population.

"Here, guv'nor – you taking everyone?" a young man chirped as he gave the captain a playful shove.

"Most people, yes. If you can walk and hold a gun, you can fight. Stand aside."

There was a little more to it than that, and this should have been done three months ago when the Lenks were first rattling their sabres. It could have been more orderly, and mobilisation might have discouraged them from landing on the dockside and attacking tenements full of ordinary people.

Zbych squeezed into the office where the recruiting sergeant was pushing back men from the table. "Any trouble, Vasya?"

At that point, one enthusiastic volunteer almost took the sergeant's spectacles off with his copy of the illustrated journal *Okno k Miru*, Window on the World, a special edition with the army's begging letter on its front cover.

Zbych shook his head and sat down, opening up another line. "Calm down," he barked. "You'll all get served."

The room hushed.

"That's better."

The sergeant turned his eyes back to his own group of men. "You must be a wonder on the parade ground, captain," he said as he handed the beetle-browed young man in front of him a card and told him to take himself to the medical officer. "You're going to need it with this lot." His lips had formed the word rabble, but he had thought better of it.

"It helps, Vasya."

"You don't sound too convinced," the sergeant replied.

*****

"I'm afraid you're too old, sir," Zbych said, looking up into the eyes of a besuited man with sagging cheeks, fiddling with his watch-chain. "We only take those under forty."

"I'm thirty-nine," the man asserted. "I've not yet turned forty and I was..." He tapped the pamphlet he carried. "Look here: '18-40 year olds'. You've got to let me join up. I was born in Syevirmetyevo. Those are my relatives, sir...It'll be short! Over by

26

Yule, they're saying! The Empire can't possibly allow the beasts to take two cities without repercussions."

Zbych took the pamphlet. Normal recruitment was up to the age of 35, but with the enemy pouring onto Krovot and Salvat soil like ants, forty was permissible. There were some men who looked to be in their late thirties in the corridor pushing their snouts into the room in quiet anxiety that by the time they got their *uniforms* it would be over. Zbych fixed the man with a stare.

It hit him right before the eyes. The man had only just turned forty-one. In fact, Zbych could read his exact date and time of birth. It came to him in a flash of light and a whirling of calendar dates, like the spinning numbers on his desk back at the barracks. 13 Sierpien, 1,930th year of the Insulan Calendar; in other words, 13 Sickle, the eighth month of the year. This was the end of Vieriesien, Heather, the ninth month.

"You've been forty-one for six weeks, haven't you?" Zbych said.

The man, who had been nervously fingering his watch-fob and had his eyes cast down, nodded.

"You do realise you'd have had to show your papers at some point," the captain said. "No getting away with it."

"But you said…"

"We're also at the mercy of the doctors," Zbych said, cursing his simplistic statement earlier on. "If they don't pass you fit, you won't be going. If you want to help, the war office will need people. A good reference from your employer and you can help fill a younger man's place at the stavka. But I suggest you remain in your current position. If the Middle Mountains are crossed or Podhalensko falls, we'll be reassessing the situation. For now, Krovt is safer than you think. The trains out are packed enough as it is."

***

Zbych had known of his talent for ordering people about, and been wary about misusing it; no-one liked a bully. But this new ability seemed to have little consequence for his reputation. He checked everyone. He had to do it consciously, but for most people the dates fell in the right place and he waved people through. After a while, the vision of a spinning calendar disappeared, and he only saw the numerals.

Some he turned down pleaded that they were terrifically fit for forty, having followed this-or-that physical culture correspondence course. Some were old soldiers themselves, decorated the last time the Lenks had been restless and had to be put in their place, but Zbych noted that one man was even carrying a cane and trying to pass himself off as fit. He got a few pugnacious women trying to pretend to be boys, but recommended that they seek employment in munitions factories further south if they could leave the city.

By the end of the day there were still people waiting, but he was permitted to clock off and hand over to another shift of officers. He walked down the line towards the entrance to the officers' mess, looking at them through these new lenses and sending a few of the too-old and too-young packing. The sergeants were normally accommodated elsewhere, but he invited Vasya to the commissioned men's refectory as a reward for his hard work. They sat down at a table, and Zbych produced a case of cigarillos. "Better than those *papirosy*."

"Yup," Vasya said.

Zbych lit a smoke, leaned back and relaxed. As his mind unravelled from the day's stress, he suddenly blinked in surprise. Each person around him now wore their date of birth on their sleeve. The mess stewards. The orderly cleaning the floor and emptying the bins. A woman draped over the arm of her aristocratic lover, who was flouting the rules and had brought her in from outside, though no-one cared. Vasya himself.

He rubbed his eyes.

Then it seemed as if everything had a birth-date. The chairs and tablecloths, the food arriving on the table. The curtains delicately screening the continuing clamour of the new recruits from view.

The mess was plastered and painted in fresh colours, but he could see the date on which that paint was applied, not that long ago according the long string of numbers unfolding across the wall. The glass on the window beyond the curtains was etched with another date, and the ceilings bore their own stamp. He gripped the table as if the room was spinning.

Vasya had his hand on Zbych's arm. "We need a glass of water," the sergeant begged of the steward who had already brought them their meal.

"17 Travien," Zbych said, nodding. He frowned.

"What? What has my birthday to do with anything?" Vasya asked.

"29 Sychen." Cutting-month.

"Is that your birthday?"

Zbych shook his head and put his hand up to his mouth, as if he had just breathed fire.

Vasya chortled. "Come on, sir, enough of this. You've been doing this all day, telling people when they were born. Let it go."

"1 Tsvetien."

"Flower-month? What's got into you?"

"25 Zhovtien!" Yellow-month.

"Knock it off, captain. You've had your joke."

Zbych put his head in his hands and tried to articulate what he thought was happening, but each time he opened his mouth, a random date came out.

The sergeant stood up and called over a steward. "Get Doctor Chislenko. He knows magic when he sees it. Maybe he'll know what's going on."

Zbych took a drink of water, hoping that this might solve the problem, but it didn't. He stood up and ran out of the room.

**

Doctor Arvid Chislenko stood over Zbych in the private consulting room. "Bit of an embarrassing problem, eh, Piech?"

Zbych nodded, dumbly. He could still see all the dates on which everything was made; the room's equipment was brand new, the bedlinen, the stethoscope, even Chislenko's chair. The Osipovo hospital had recently been upgraded at vast expense. A couple of friends had complained that the money had gone to the army rather than the shabby public infirmary in Krasnaya Polyana. In amongst his fear at the runaway talent, he was curious as to what he'd see there if he dared look.

"Well, don't worry about this being permanent," the doctor said in his pinched voice. "You're not mad. Just under the influence, so to speak, of what happens when we forget magic is a tool rather than a crutch."

Zbych smirked and coughed.

"It'll wear off overnight. I could put you out with valeriate if you want."

The captain opened his mouth, and then realised what might happen if he spoke. So he reached for a scrap of paper on the doctor's desk, manufactured on 9 Sierpien the previous year. *4 Krasien 12 Bieriesien 6 Liutiy* he wrote.

"Nice handwriting," Chislenko observed.

Zbych flung the pencil across the room.

"Temper, temper. You're a grown man, not a little boy. Nod for yes, shake your head for no. Now, would you like to go to sleep now? To save yourself from further humiliation?"

Zbych nodded.

Doctor Chislenko gave a cold smile and mixed up a glass of sedative. "Go and get ready for bed, and for goodness sake don't try and communicate with anyone. I'll let the brass know what's happened."

***

"Will I be able to do that again?" Zbych asked the doctor a few days later, the next time they ran into each other in the mess. The recruitment surge continued, and men were awaiting dispatch to the front. The regular army was holding Podhalensko, but the Lenks had reached the Kila at Paszynsko in Salvatka, eighty versts from Krovt, where an artillery battalion had held the Krovot bank, making an old fort into a new one and preventing the enemy from crossing the river.

"You mean determine someone's age just from looking at them?"

Zbych nodded. As Chislenko had prophesied, the night's sleep had done him good and he had been hoarse but speaking properly in the morning.

"You still have that ability, but a magician must keep control of his talents," Chislenko said with a curt nod. "There's a reason you don't like to bark orders at people, isn't there?"

"I want people to love and respect me. I read about how Bulovkin cultivated his regiment and gained their loyalty through kindness rather than fear."

"But they won't if you make a fool or a bully of yourself. Am I right?"

Zbych took a drink of his tea. "You're right."

"Good man," Chislenko said, with a smile, warmer this time.

THE AMBUSH

The Ambush

Scouting through the delta swampland was something assigned to the lowest, most expendable grunts. Corporal Solinski knew that Lieutenant Staunton, back in his nice cabin in Vassilinsk, was taking advantage of the peasants' gratitude on being liberated, while he, his ne'er-do-well brother-in-law Kurak and several other under-enthusiastic miscreants were out here, shivering in the mud under the surveillance of Lenkish soldiers. They hadn't found anything of consequence, and were about to go home in disgrace.

"Bloody w---- of a goddess!" Kurak yelled from the riverbank.

Solinski stalked over, angry at this unnecessary noise and expecting to find that Kurak had fallen in.

Branches snapped nearby, and the other men fell in behind him and took out their guns, just in case. He put his hand on his pistol – and his mouth fell open.

A mammoth, bark-brown creature stood before them in the river, dripping with moss and leaf-litter, with a nose like an oozing gutter-pipe, and mis-shapen, green teeth in a partly-open mouth.

It waded towards them as if every step was painful.

Kurak was cowering on the bank, hiding his face. The creature, some sort of forest spirit but clearly visible to them all, stepped out of the river, reaching out its hands towards Kurak, each one big enough to grasp a man's torso in its fist. Solinski heard a burst of gunfire, and instinctively fired his own pistol towards it, blinded by fear.

He heard his brother-in-law's screams cut off with a thud and a whimper. A knot of enemy soldiers had launched themselves upon them as they had stood insensible with fear at the creature's appearance.

The creature looked reproachfully at them and shambled onwards unhurt.

Solinski knew what the enemy would do to him if he didn't also get out there very quickly, so he took off back towards the road.

THE MESMERIST

The Mesmerist

*O*ur *lips meet, his moustache soft against my nose. I squeeze his belly against mine; I can feel his heart beating. He ruffles my hair with his hand.*

It's the first time I've been with a gentleman. I don't think I'll ever forget the way it feels to be in a relationship with an equal. It's not easy to submit to one of your own kind when you're used to being in command, but I love him enough to do it for him.

I bend down and open the buttons of his trousers.

"Keeping you up are we, Lieutenant?" the magician rasped.

Guffaws came from the gaggle of tanked-up men in the front row of the Paszynsko barracks auditorium, and Jerzy Zakowski felt his cheeks burst with shame at his private fantasy. The heaviness of his head reminded him that he'd also nearly fallen asleep, giving evidently giving grave offence to the performer engaged to entertain the troops. This wiry little man wore a suit stained with flash-powder and a malevolent smile that revealed crooked teeth. His tricks had been sleight of hand, of which it was easy to divine the methods.

"Lisak's tail, these nobs, eh? In a world of their own and no mistake. Now this, lads, is a trick that doesn't use sleight of hand."

Jerzy raised an eyebrow. Sceptical mutterings came from other members of the audience.

The entertainer pulled a silver watch from his pocket. "I promise you, this is genuine magic. I don't do this for everyone, but, seeing as it's your lieutenant's birthday" – he winked at Jerzy – "an' he's prob'ly spending it pretty far away from his Mamma, let me conjure up summat for him…"

Jerzy slunk down inside his uniform, desperately wanting to get back to his private quarters and go to bed. He'd come here to lift his spirits and forget himself, not to be humiliated in front of private soldiers.

Gerald and I are together, naked, on my bed. He lies on his front and I give him a rub-down. The door is locked, but everyone knows that, be it a man or a woman with me, an officer is allowed his privacy. We can explore each other's bodies to our hearts' content. He calls me "George" - I've tried to coach him on how to pronounce "Jerzy", to no avail.

He turns me over to massage my back. "You must get so bored with only the peasants and their disapproval for company."

"Well, I was at the lyceum in Krovt only two years ago," I say. "We had plenty of opportunities for satisfaction there, but not much for love."

Jerzy had expected the conjurer to be about to produce a bouquet of roses or a rabbit from his hat as an inappropriate gift for him. The watch began to flick backwards and forwards, glinting in the gaslight. The room quietened all of a sudden, the men at the front having done most of the heckling each falling quiet in turn.

He took a deep breath as he too felt first giddy, and then calm detachment from the mortal world. This was certainly no conjuring trick; this wasn't even a conventional séance, where a shaman might call spirits forward to speak with a conscious audience. Instead, he felt his spirit pulled from his body into what must be the Beyond: the realm of the spirits themselves.

"I've been sent up the Kila," Gerald says, taking a drag on his cigarillo. "Von Hipplersdorf ordered us to find a safe route through the hills towards Mogilyovka. They've put a POW camp right on top of the peasants' charnel house there and it's my job to sweep the place for beetles."

He means the Lenks – the enemy. "When will you be back?"

"Not until we can see the perimeter fence there and report back," Gerald snorts. "Like me and a few clodhoppers are going to overpower a whole division of maniacs who crucify children."

He laughs so hard I can see his tonsils.

He found himself standing in a mountain village, downstream along the Kila. Around him were the ruins of houses, their brick stoves standing up through collapsed, charred walls, pointing accusingly at the sky. Remains of soldiers' tents, also burned, littered the road. From the trees hung several figures – a female priest, the wise-man and probably the starosta or village elder and his wife. They were not long dead, but as they twisted in the breeze, Jerzy knew there was no way to save them.

He'd seen this before in villages left by the retreating enemy. They herded captives back towards the cities after executing any local dignitaries and remaining soldiery.

Gerald.

He reached for his pistol and moved cautiously up the street.

The coward can't even look at me when he's talking.

When I demand to know how Gerald died, Corporal Solinski just shrugs. "I didn't see it. We were ambushed and we couldn't have defended Vassilinsk properly – there weren't enough of us left to fall back there."

I tell myself to take hold of myself and not pursue the matter. A relationship such as mine is not forbidden unless it would be fraternisation between the ranks, though I know a number of men take lovers from the ranks and make them their batmen in order to disguise what they're doing. But even so, I don't want salacious rumours going round my company that their commander lost his boyfriend. I have to remain firm. Death is around every corner – it was Gerald the other day; it could be me tomorrow.

Solinski lost his brother-in-law out there too. There are rumours that the Lenks distracted them with a terrible apparition – sorcery? – and so no-one has been punished for deserting their commanding officer. Solinski would have been shot in the early days of this war.

If I let myself go to pieces, I'll let everyone else down too.

Jerzy wandered around the ruined township, trying to suppress the anger and pity he felt for the dead and focus on why the magician had sent him here. When he put his hand out to anything within the area, he realised he was closing his hand around thin air. He could only look, not touch.

He came to a cottage that had a stronger structure than the wooden peasant huts and was not so easily destroyed by fire. Although he could not open the door by normal means, he found he could simply float through the walls. It appeared to be a small *stavka*; from the décor, it had been located in the starosta's dwelling, the officer in charge bunking with the elder and his family.

Groans came from beneath an overturned bookcase. Jerzy quickly sped round to the far side and found Gerald lying on the floor, his face contorted in pain and his throat choking and spluttering. Blood seeped out from beneath the solid oak dresser.

He couldn't even mop his lover's brow or hold his hand during his last moments. Determined to feel like he was doing something, he folded his incorporeal hand around Gerald's outstretched palm, its fingers twitching as the muscles went into spasm.

"You came to me," he said, groaning. "Are you dead too? Have they taken Paszynsko? How did they kill you?" He choked and his head rolled to one side, but Jerzy could see that he was still conscious.

"I'm alive. I was granted this vision by one of those mesmerist chaps. Vassilinsk fell a week ago, but Paszynsko hasn't fallen – it doesn't look like they've got the men to attack us."

Gerald tried to speak, but nothing more came out. He jerked his head back in the last throes of death. Jerzy stood up to leave his body in peace, but as he turned to leave the cottage, he saw a spectral figure get up from the floor and come towards him.

"It's a bit more than a vision, George."

Jerzy embraced him, hugging and kissing. As they began to get more intimate with each other, Gerald's form dissipated slowly but surely, until he was consumed by light.

This was *goodbye*.

As his lover left him, Vassilinsk itself faded. Jerzy found himself back into the room where he had begun his journey, biting his lip and wondering whether he had overstepped the boundaries spirit had set for him – whether Gerald would have lasted longer in his embrace if he hadn't started to fool around. The other men were less vocal now, each looking furtive and restless, as if they had seen similar visions.

"I thought that'd get your attention," the mesmerist said. "You ain't alone when you're with your brothers-in-arms. Everyone has someone they need to say goodbye to. Whatever you would have done with him, his time was up."

Jerzy rubbed his eyes and stood up to leave. "Thank you. If you'd excuse me – it's been a long day and I've got to get an early start tomorrow. Thank you."

A PIECE OF
THEIR SOUL

A Piece of Their Soul

William Latimer wiped the photograph of his son Arnold, hanging above the staircase, as he had done for the past year. He never let dust settle on his sons' portraits, cleaning them every evening after he returned from work.

As he rubbed the glass this evening, however, there was a sudden, stabbing pain in his belly. Doubled over, his foot missed the step, and he fell, reaching out for the bristly, foot-worn drugget and the smooth floor beneath it. An acrid smell filled his nostrils, the sickening odour of smoke from explosives familiar to him from the public works he'd overseen as a young surveyor's apprentice. For several moments he heard voices speaking in unfamiliar languages, the sound of gunfire and more recognisable artillery barrages. Then a heavy blow came to the back of his head, and he found himself face down in phantom mud, tasting it between his teeth, feeling it underneath his fingernails – yet not seeing it on the stair in front of him.

His wife Alice was suddenly at the bottom of the bannister and speedily coming up the staircase. She put her hand on his shoulder. "William, what happened?"

He got up, shaking his head, the sensation vanishing. He looked at his wife, wondering whether she would accept a magical explanation, because there was no other reason for his experience. "How did that happen?" he murmured, to himself rather than directly addressing his wife. "What did I do different today?"

Alice shrugged. "You're not hurt?"

"No." He looked at her, and then back at the portrait of Arnold.

"Was it something…"

"I believe so," he said quietly, and explained what exactly had transpired. "It was like being hit by lightning."

Arnold had attained the rank of corporal not long before his capture – long enough to send them home a portrait, but not for him to get leave to come home and see them. He alone of Latimer's three sons had attained any rank; Philip and Edward had been early casualties, their own pictures taken before they had even been dispatched from the training camp at Morley Point to the front, almost a thousand miles north. The couple had received notification of their deaths in one of the first pushes, had grieved, and accepted that fate.

But for two years of the three the war had been in progress, they had hoped that Arnold might survive. Everything had been over now for eight months, the Lenkish enemy pushed back to their own country across the Eastern Straits and subjected to occupation. They now only had one daughter, Astrid, currently away visiting her aunt in Carstead, ten miles upriver along the Bree, anxious to meet a sturdy farmer who might consider her a good bride.

However, from what the ministry had said in the ominous telegram they received, it seemed his death in the POW camp at Mogilyovka would have involved some form of torture. They avoided any details of how their son might have died, but Latimer's pain had come from his gut. The earthy taste in his mouth suggested that his son might have been on his knees, only to have been kicked in the back of the head and stamped into the ground. From what he had witnessed of injuries in the course of public works, he could fill in the gaps in the dying man's viewpoint.

He reached out and touched the picture again, but felt nothing odd – only glass at room temperature.

Alice took the rag from her husband's hands. "It's not a good idea to go tempting the spirits, William – if that's what it was and you didn't just trip."

He looked at her and shook his head. "I'm positive it was his spirit. No simple accident could account for the smells; not in here, at least."

"My mother used to say that photographs took – stole – a piece of a person's soul," Alice said, almost in a whisper. "Many of the old folks in Carstead grumbled about the evil eye when the rector set up a camera to take their portraits. They said the gods would destroy him for his acts of sorcery and witchcraft, and a man of the cloth was sure to be first in line for punishment of that sort."

"And?"

"He did die in a sanatorium." She shrugged. "Mind you, enough people get touched on the lungs for it to have been in any way to do with stealing other people's souls through a purely mechanical process."

"Give me back the rag," he said.

Alice handed it to him slowly. "Don't provoke it, William. You know you're not supposed to meddle in things you can't control. I'll fetch the cunning-man tomorrow and have him come to look at the portraits."

"No. If the portraits are possessed, I won't let you take my boys from me a second time. I've never felt anything but comfort when I look at their pictures...until today." He blew the dust off the black ribbon threaded through the cheap filigree frames, which seemed to have settled even since he had wiped the glass, and carefully ran it along the metal fretwork, with no untoward experiences.

He began to think he had simply imagined the occurrence, but it still seemed real, and he could think of no other reason he had slipped on the carpet, carefully positioned and kept secured by the stair-rods. He was careful at work and at home, going out of his way to protect his much-diminished family. He made sure the civil construction sites he worked on were not going to ruin the health or safety of his workers, to whom the Department of Public Works paid rather generous pensions if they were injured in the course of duty. He was unusual in this regard, but Latimer knew the moral – and spiritual – consequences of letting his workforce down. A haunted site was a distressing place to work for someone aware of ghosts.

"No-one is going to take your boys away from you, William. No-one can take the memories we have of them." She shuddered. "But the idea of having…ghosts…in the house… What if they haven't gone to the light?"

"If they are trapped in there," Latimer started, "then…" He paused. "This is preposterous. We've had photographs taken with no ill-effect on us. I've never felt anything in the front room from the pictures of your parents, who both died in their beds. I occasionally converse with my mother, but not while in front of her portrait."

"I want to consult the shaman," Alice insisted. "Or I want you to take the pictures down. We still have small plates of them before the war. Your fascination is morbid."

Latimer turned away. A fleeting smell of explosives came to him again. He began to think why it was today the spirits had chosen to send him this encounter. He counted back. Mogilyovka had been liberated a few weeks before Yule. They'd seen bodies still hanging from trees, their flesh long since stripped bare – the illustrated newspapers, ghouls all of them, had prepared engravings that had gone into excruciating visual detail, although they couldn't easily portray such sensations. Those prisoners still on their feet had described the indescribable; Latimer knew some of it was exaggerated to whip up hatred against the Lenks, but the occupiers had done enough to convince the inhabitants of the occupied provinces and soldiers liberated from their captivity that there was substance to the stories of abuse. Thousands of individuals couldn't be singing from the same propaganda broadsheets prepared in Galistow, Achava, Krovt and Ludlin. There was no ability to print photographs in papers, but he'd spoken to men at work who'd seen the front, if not the camps.

He thought back to the smoke and the stabbing pain in the gut. A bayonet, most likely. He realised he had allowed anger to well in his throat, and feared turning round to unleash it on his wife. When a man at work didn't put in an honest day's labour, he felt the same thing. "Public charges" – workhouse inmates, mostly former vagrants to have been there while so able to work – who were foisted upon him by the department to clear land ready for the free navvies to come in tasted a different side to William Latimer than the pleasant and concerned boss.

It was all he could do to hand the rag back to Alice and walk away upstairs, where she heard him sobbing within five minutes.

The photographs remained on the wall. Every time Alice mentioned getting the shaman in to look at them or a priest to bless them, she was met by insistence that to disturb them would be to disturb the boys. Although after that Latimer felt presences on the stairs when he went up to bed, he never had a shock from the pictures again, and gradually the experience faded from his mind.

MOGILYOVKA

Mogilyovka

From the notes of Franciszek Lipkowski, ethnographer and folklorist, 1,969ᵗʰ year, Insulan Calendar.

All human beings are inclined to adapt their lifestyle to the terrain, and the peasants of the Kila delta are no exception. Boreal marshland presents an instability in the soil which presents a known difficulty to securing the foundations in the city of Syevirmetyevo, but also has been found to cause problems with the burial of the dead. Corpses surface readily after a month or two in the silt, and so traditional burials, with important people buried with grave-goods ripe to rot or be robbed when they float to the surface, are virtually unknown.

I travelled to the region myself to observe the funeral of a particular shaman, Vassilisa Smaragdova, a great ascetic who wandered the delta region proclaiming the coming of the apocalypse. What set her apart from the simply mad hedge prophets was that she did this in many degrees of frost in only the simplest of monastic garb. Her funeral in Mogilyovka – which means *Gravestown* – was attended by hundreds.

Even if Smaragdova had been the daughter of a landowner or peasant mayor, she would still have been buried in a simple shift. Unlike others elsewhere who will not violate a corpse lest they wound the soul in the next life, the peasants here do not believe that, after death, the human body possesses any special relevance. It is waste which might pollute drinking water if left to fester in the ground. Smaragdova was transported on a simple litter to the site by the elders of the village where she grew up, naked apart from the shift to protect her dignity; it would be wrong to waste good cloth on the marsh. As the foothills of the Middle Mountains rise beyond

Mogilyovka, the ground is firmer and can take the bodies of modern townspeople without regurgitating them. For centuries, the peasants of the region have brought their dead to large boulders littering the sides of the road.

Accordingly, we tramped a verst from the road towards the river itself, and found a suitable rock on which to lay the shaman to rest. A priest said a few dry words, and then we left. A simple ceremony, conducted by simple people, for a simple person. Scavenging birds wheeling overhead indicated what would happen next.

Public health officials now forbid this practice in most ordinary cases, insisting on earth burials, and so there were no other corpses surrounding the slab on which Smaragdova was laid to await her fate. I returned the following morning to see what might have happened in the night, and what a person eaten by buzzards might look like. I saw the ground churned up by the many booted feet, so I knew it was the right one, but it was empty. By the rock, I saw a single print from a naked foot. It is said some holy people do not decompose in death; but Smaragdova had ascended to Minerva. Her body was too good for this world to simply be treated as rubbish.

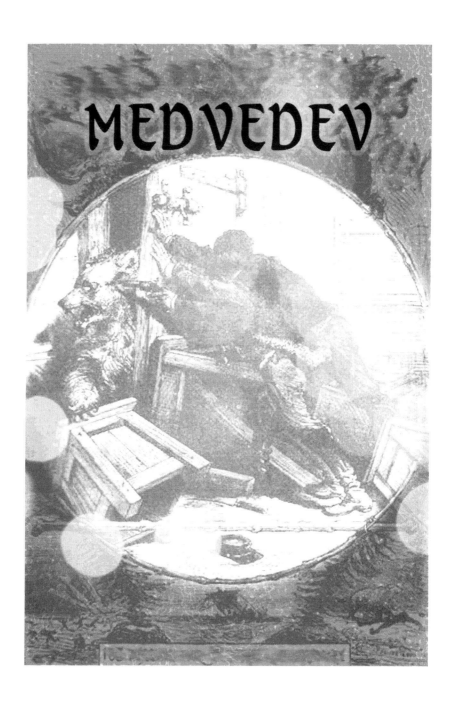

Medvedev

Sergei Medvedev could see his three children, Lara, Foma and Mitya out of the window in the courtyard below, playing in the late spring evening, the sun low on the city's horizon. The sun didn't set until very late in the evening, so Medvedev could work late without having to light a lamp. Since the death of his wife Shura, Lara as the lady of the house now should really have been helping cook and clean, but she still wandered off to play too easily and forgetfully. If she was to go into service, Medvedev thought, he'd have to make sure she knew the basic household routine inside out; he'd have to start keeping her indoors.

Let them play, he thought. *While they still have a chance.*

He turned back to the pile of leather in front of him and began to cut out the new pair of shoes. The absence of his wife was still gnawing away; he wouldn't deny that he had a temper on him of late. If he thought about it much, which he tried not to, he would have said that he missed Shura with sorrow that penetrated much of his current life. It didn't affect his job, because he lost himself in his craft during the day, but he'd retreated into the house away from Lavrov and Petrov and the others. He wouldn't take beer or vodka because he was afraid he'd drink too much.

Like most working men who lost their wives it was the day-to-day things that he missed. His shirts were never clean; his dinner was bland and tasteless, and even overcooked when Lara forgot to watch it. He was busy trying to make the shoes that kept the family fed, clothed and housed and needed someone else to keep an eye on the housework. He was proud of his work and was looking forward to the income from his dozy daughter's first place as someone's kitchenmaid. With one boy earning a factory wage and one boy helping him with his trade he could probably breathe a bit easier and save towards Mitya's premium, whilst Foma was apprenticed to him for nothing. He'd have to get better at cooking once his daughter left him or find another wife, but he could manage with her for now. Oleg Aksentiyev's wife Vasilisa sent down her pelmeni once a week, and he always found a way to repay her using his own skills as a tailor and cobbler, and occasionally sent his daughter up to scrub their floors. Aksentiyev had two rooms and even a bath-tub, and was the only person in the entire building who still softened Medvedev's anger with a few words of comfort and wisdom to lighten the gloom.

From outside came sudden shouts. Medvedev ran to the window to see his sons quarrelling with two of the other boys from another flat in the tenement building. It was just outside his window; they were on the ground floor. Foma was wrestling with little Anton Petrov and Mitya was trying to pull Tolik Shurichkin off him. Lara ran in to the room, anxious to warn her father about what was going on, but Medvedev was already rolling up his sleeves and telling her off for not coming in sooner to look at the pot, and that he couldn't work and cook at the same time. The girl, not more than nine, scurried over to the range and looked in at the stew, while her angry father stormed out into the yard. The boys got into fights occasionally; both the elder Petrov and Shurichkin had told him off for not keeping a proper eye on his sons.

As a craftsman rather than a factory labourer he couldn't manage everything at once; even if he sat facing his window he always had his eyes on his work. Other men could come home, have their dinner on the table and their wife smiling at them, and their children weren't left to their own devices to get into scraps because their mothers were always out gossiping in the courtyard. It wasn't easy for most of the men but they managed because their wives were there to handle it for them.

He gave his sons hell.

He dragged Foma in first, and then pulled Mitya off Tolik. In full view of the rest of the boys, he dragged his son inside by the ear.

Little Shurichkin backed off, surprised at old Medvedev's reaction to playful wrestling, and Petrov's son ran back to his own family's rooms crying when Medvedev boxed his ears for good measure, extracting a shout of anger out of his mother. "You should be doing that," he growled at Lada, who wiped away her son's tears with her pinnie and glared at him.

His own boys were unable to pacify him at all. He knocked them about, dragging them through into the room. He shut the door and took off his belt.

Lara cowered back towards the range, hastily spooning through the stew. In a small voice she said, "It's all right, pa, the meat isn't cooked through yet and I've still got to cut up the cabbage."

"Shut up," Medvedev bellowed.

He struck both the boys with the belt. It wasn't the carefully dealt out smacks that most parents gave their children. It was a ferocious whipping, which left Mitya trying to crawl under the table. Medvedev growled and grunted, angry. "When I tell you not to scrap, I mean it."

"Pa, stop," Lara begged.

Medvedev turned on her. "I told you to keep an eye on them, but I bet you were gossiping with Sveta and Anya, weren't you?"

Lara yelped as her father struck her on the face. Although a good clout from a man his size might well draw blood, he felt the rake of an animal's paw, like a cat but bigger and more forceful. She looked at the hand he had raised to her and screamed – he had grown claws and those claws had scratched her face deeply. She ran for the door, but he blocked the way.

Mitya and Foma could see what had happened to their father too. He no longer felt human; he had turned into a giant brown bear, snarling and grunting. Trapped inside this body, blood, cloth, leather, tools and even stew were spilled and clawed at in the small room. Lara ended up pinned beneath her father's paws, his claws tearing into more of her skin; he tried to tear himself away, but his rage had consumed him. Mitya got out of the door and called for help from the neighbours, before the were-bear dragged him back into the room. Foma scrambled underneath the table and escaped the terrible vengeance of the bewildered animal in the room, though he was only barely managing to hold it off by the time hurrying footsteps could be heard outside the door.

Petrov and Lavrov had just returned from work. Coming in the front door, they heard the frightened, bleeding Mitya. Medvedev had cornered Foma, and Lara was unconscious, bleeding from the bear's claws and teeth and burnt by the stew. Petrov took up a poker and thrust it into the range, but the bear realised what they could do and he felt the shape fading in their angry gaze.

He sat there in the middle of the room, inconsolable. He begged his two friends to be merciful, telling them he hadn't touched Tolik or Anton, only his own children. Lavrov ran to fetch a constable and a doctor, leaving Petrov to try and soothe the poor shoemaker, who cradled his daughter, the worst hurt, pleading with the heavens not to let her die.

WHERE THE DEVIL
SAYS GOODNIGHT

Where the Devil Says Goodnight

The gloomy evening pressed in around the drawing room of Dwor Kruczewski. Despite it being two months off the solstice, and still light after dinner, no-one was in the mood for leaving the house. Leszek Pawlicki had gone to Panczewo to visit relatives, leaving his wife to keep her father company. Halina had not come down for dinner again, for the fourth night in a row.

"Have you contacted Carrie yet, Papa?" Celina asked.

"I'm in two minds whether I ought to go down," the old squire said, poker in hand, absent-mindedly stoking the fire. With the sun descending, there was a need for a fire. "With your mother in such a state I can't abandon her, and there's always work to be done on the estate. How long can you stay with us?"

"Leszek needs to be back in Lvinsk in a week's time. Someone telegraphed him about an employee allegedly embezzling from us, and…"

"If I'm to go anywhere, I need you to stay here and look after your Mamma," he said. "Leszek will need to go home if that is the case, but you might stay, surely? A big store like that can run itself without the owner's wife being present."

Celina fingered her prayer-rope, in her pocket, and appeared to think for a moment. Her father observed her face go through a range of expressions; on previous form, she might take a full day to make up her mind.

"It might be best if we left you to this," she said eventually.

"If Michal's wife had stayed with him, then he might not have wandered off," the squire snapped. "You have responsibilities to us as well as to your husband. You can't hide in Lvinsk while the estate is on such perilous ground."

"If I remember correctly, it was he who claimed *she* was being unfaithful to him."

"Well, quite. She ought to have taken her duties to her husband more seriously."

"Does a woman owe her allegiance to the first man to ask it of her? By that argument I should go home with Leszek immediately."

"I'd have expected it of Michal too," Wladek added hastily. "He made mistakes."

Celina still gave him a look that could curdle milk. "I'm in the way here, Papa," she replied. "Let me take Mamma home with us. She'd enjoy the sea air and leave you free to go to Ludlin to sort out his affairs."

Wladek considered her suggestion; it sounded like a good compromise. He unfolded himself from his arm-chair and got up. "Speaking of her, it's time I went to her. If she won't come down here, then I shouldn't abandon her completely."

Halina Piechowa had not left her apartments, still less the house, since Killian Bailey had written to them that Michal was missing. It was not through insipid self-pity that she stayed out of sight, nor through the expectations of a woman in mourning for her son.

Wladek crept upstairs, through the corridors of the great manor house, to his wife's study. He remembered his grandfather having the carpets laid on the stairs to prevent echoes and warm the place through the hard winters, but wooden beams and dark furniture sucked the light from the surroundings even at the best of times. He had seen the palazzos other families had constructed out of their old homes, putting in wide windows and smooth marble balustrades and staircases, but had always thought the Dwor a comfortable rather than fashionable place. To rip it apart just because he was grieving seemed drastic, but somehow necessary.

He knocked.

"Enter." The first word of any substance she had spoken to him all day.

"My dear…" he began, pushing down on the handle and opening the door.

Her study held a large library of spiritual magic and on folklore, the subject of her thesis from their days at university together. There was a desk at which she normally sat to work, but this evening she sat on the day-bed, papers spread about the room with occult symbols on them, not something she usually examined unless she was studying. A dirty teacup was upended on the table, a page nearby stained.

Littering the bed were playing cards from the couple's set for bridge, a notebook and pencil, and a slim pamphlet entitled *The Meanings of the Cards: Instructions for the Amateur Oracle.* Her face contorted in pain and desperation as she focused hard on the pattern the cards were making on the bed.

He watched her for a few minutes in silence. There was a shimmer from the cards; out of respect for his wife's beliefs, Wladek had not had his fortune told since his marriage, but he'd never seen a fairground witch conjure such a glow. Cards were sold on the understanding that anyone, even those without magical or spiritual talent, could read them through intuition and interpretation of stock meanings alone, but his wife must be channeling her own magic into those scraps of paper, trying to demand the spirits tell her what she wanted to know — to explain the reading for her rather than using the symbolism and meanings contained in the booklet.

She suddenly let go with a sob. The glow faded and she threw the cards on the floor.

Wladek finally managed to speak. "Why do you need those? Surely it's *sorcery* to try and divine like that. You've always said that…"

She fixed him with a stare, looking as alien as if she were possessed by an evil spirit or homunculus; the words choked in his throat. "I know he's not dead; he's alive somewhere in Ludlin. But I must know where *exactly* he is." Shamans did not need cards or books purchased from back-street printers. He had seen her conduct séances which brought spirits so close to the mortal world that their faces could be witnessed in the room by people who had no talent for seeing them normally. He shook his head and came further into the room, closing the door. "The spirits will not tell you where he is?"

She gestured tiredly at the notebook. "I lack the means to get to the truth through other methods. If the gods' grace will tell me nothing about my son, then I must consult the Devil and learn his ways."

"You give others clear enough messages that their loved ones are in spirit or in the Thrice-Nine Kingdoms." He fingered the black armband around his tweed jacket where its edge had become twisted. "If Michal has not been seen in three weeks, then he may not have survived. With the money I am offering for his safe return, even the worst scoundrel must be tempted. I would even forgive anyone who had harmed him if I could just see him again."

"I fear the man who has done this already believed that he will profit more from robbery and keeping quiet than from the reward."

"You can tell all that from a pack of cards?"

"I am trying to understand the fragments spirit is giving me, both through cards and other means. They talk about a mortal prison rather than immortal rest, but do not tell me where he is kept or who has imprisoned him, other than that I will meet them when the time is right."

"Then perhaps it you are not meant to know until then. That gives me hope we will eventually lay him to rest."

"He is not in the light. The spirits mentioned 'where the Devil says goodnight', and I am trying to ascertain what they mean. I even intend to visit Antonia Kolinska, but I am afraid to go crawling to her when I have been so rude to her in the past."

"I don't think that's a good idea. You have spoken out so much against Kolinska that she may not even entertain you, let alone tell you anything."

The phrase the spirits were taunting her with was common idiom, meaning a remote or desolate place. Wladek was at present more concerned that she planned to visit a local fortune-teller who made a back-street living in Panczewo. Michal had visited her tent at the local fair years ago with a friend, before moving south, and been spooked so badly his mother had tried to run the woman out of town.

"I ought to make peace with her."

"More like demand why she hexed our son," Wladek grumbled. "But I have never interfered with your work. If you truly think Michal is alive, then try and find him using what tools you have your disposal. I'll go and scour the city for him in person. Otherwise pray for him to reach the light and set our minds at rest."

He took her in his arms, but she did not want comforting; she wanted knowledge, and he couldn't give it to her. He told her of Celina's idea. "I need to arrange a place to stay in Ludlin, but I think *you* need a vacation. I plan to ask Caroline and Alexei if I might stay with them. I fancy it would be unwise to remain alone at the Hytherton house with only my valet. If someone did abduct or kidnap Michal, they might come looking at the house."

"Very well." Halina asked for a week in which to wrap up her affairs and visit the Panczewo witch before joining her daughter on the eastern coast.

***

Wodopadna Street was about as far from Dwor Kruczewski as you could get. The Zolta, or Yellow, Dniewa, named after the silt it carried down from the foothills of the Eastern Spine on its sinuous path, wound through the back streets of Panczewo. The older part of the town was now the back streets, abandoned to slide slowly into the mud. The street's name, Waterfall, was an accurate forecast of its ultimate fate; what might save it was the bridge it ran over, Mostek Wodopadny, but even then a greenshirt was always posted on its bank, making sure traffic passed over it one vehicle at a time. When the militia eventually abandoned it, it would crumble.

Halina's carriage clattered down over it, with the spring sun glinting off the mudflat beyond the inadequate stone parapet, and stopped outside a shabby stone tenement, grimy windows etched with the name ANTONIA KOLINSKA, mildew obscuring the end of the name.

"Are you sure, ma'am?" the coachman asked.

"I'm sure," she said. "If you're concerned about how this looks, wait for me at the top of the road." She got out. Almost as soon as she had, her driver pulled the reins and set off back up the road into town.

Beside the door, Halina could just about make out the word for witch. She herself had come dressed plainly, with a black mantilla draped across her bonnet and shoulders for privacy. Crossing herself to ward off evil spirits and then feeling rather ashamed for assuming the worst about the woman she was about to grace with her present, she pushed the door open, steeling herself.

The house was small and rather dirty; Kolinska evidently made little money from her talents. Halina blinked until her eyes became accustomed to the gloom, and rang the bell on the counter, holding the handle lightly as if it was red hot. She then removed the veil from her high-crowned bonnet. Although she wanted to be discreet, there was no sense in hiding herself from Kolinska.

The old woman entered the front room, and her face turned sour. "You've come to me, Madame Piech? To what do I owe the honour?"

Halina shook her head, gravely. "I was wrong, Antonia. Forgive me. He's not in the light. Spirit tells me he is still alive, but I cannot find him."

"We both agree your son has a destiny. I told him that myself a few years ago."

Halina tried to hold back the thought that Kolinska had actually cursed her son; she knew better than many people that fortune-tellers merely told people their future, rather than forced them to undergo a fate of their choosing. "Destiny is a mountain. There are many paths up it. If Michal has gone for a reason, then I need to know it in order to put my mind at rest."

"And what gives you the right to peace of mind?" Kolinska snapped. "What makes you so special?" She sat down at her old desk and unlocked a drawer in it, withdrawing some battered cards. "Draw one."

Halina fumbled with her purse. "How much?"

"Your word of honour that you will cease slandering me to others and afford me some of the dignity you keep to yourself. Stop calling me a blasphemer because I do not subscribe to your narrow view of the Goddess' will."

"Minerva will determine our fates. She wove them Herself long before we were born, and she is the only one who knows exactly what will happen to Michal."

"So why do you not take comfort from that?"

Halina swallowed and took a card, her hand trembling. It was the Devil, an image of the ancient thunder-god Piorun dispensing justice. The interloper god. Everyone had different names for him, but he was the same entity to everyone, just like the four deities – mother, father, brother, sister – making up the holy family.

"Come on! I haven't got all day! Another three cards."

Halina turned over the Sorcerer, the Sundering, and the Angel.

"There we go. Fate has spoken. We see a tiny part of the Goddess' tapestry. As I told your son and his friend when they saw me together, one will die and be reborn, one will die in battle, and one will be king of his own country – or Governor, as you will." Contempt continued to drip from her voice, and Halina lowered her gaze to the cards. "But the Angel more clearly tells me what will happen to Michal within the space of a year or two. It's not your place to interfere, but you need to seek out his saviour to truly put your mind at rest."

"So this is where he becomes…" Halina's voice cracked in trepidation. This was no clearer than her own séances. "The spirits told me he was 'where the devil says goodnight'."

Kolinska looked up at Halina but said nothing. She took her cards back, shuffled them, and replaced them in the drawer. "Your time is up. I can't answer for spirits; you know I can't. I hear them only fleetingly, which is why I use the cards to focus. I still can't tell you whether Michal is the one that rules, or whether he is the one who dies."

Halina whisked her mantilla over her face, which was already flushed, her throat tight and choking. A dull headache was coming on, the atmosphere in the room souring like milk on a summer's day. She turned from Kolinska, taking her smelling salts out of her purse and taking a few deep breaths of the pungent hartshorn underneath the veil. She could feel the witch's stare on the back of her neck, and then turned round, very slowly and deliberately.

"Don't come the innocent with me. I think you know the spirits better than that," she snapped. "You talk to them and you tell people exactly what they say. That was why you were excommunicated, not because of those parlour tricks you turn with your cards."

The reference was deliberate. Kolinska looked thunderstruck. "I am not a…if you think…I'll have you know it was only once, when I was hungry and homeless, something you'll hopefully never have to experience. The shaming on my knees in church lasted longer than the pleasure of it all."

Halina turned away. "I'm sorry for what happened. I had no idea…I'm sorry, I spoke out of turn."

"No-one has much idea how difficult it is to keep your virtue when there's practicality at stake. You're the one trying to turn tricks for a scrap of knowledge."

She was right. The goddess had shown her grace already, and she'd ignored it in the pursuit of worldly knowledge. Minerva was asking her to have patience; she'd agreed to go to the seaside with Celina because she might get some physical rest there, but she knew the mental distress would follow her to Lvinsk, and another reading would hardly set her mind at rest until she was reunited with her son. "It's patience I need, not knowledge," she said stiffly, still in a sulky daze, hot with the frustrated anger of someone who knew what was good for them but still had trouble accepting it.

She wiped her eyes on her veil before Kolinska saw her tears.

"Turn to me," Kolinska sighed. "I'm sorry for your loss,"

Halina turned back round at the sound of a friendlier voice.

Kolinska held out her hands and the squire's wife realised after a few seconds' pause she was meant to take them. "They've put him out of reach of you and Pan Wladyslaw," she said, seeming to concentrate all her energies. "It's up to the Angel to make the next move, but he's already in there doing the will of the gods, even though he doesn't know quite what he's doing or why. You can find your son in spirit, but he hasn't left this world — in fact, I promise you will see him again. But for now you must wait — whatever magic your son's captor wields, it is too strong. He will simply turn it on others, and he has few of your honest scruples about using it. That former wife of Michal's…Madame Caroline, am I right? She is at his mercy."

The séance seemed to drain Kolinska, and she sank back into her chair, rubbing her hands and arms, and blinking as if her eyes were sore. Halina knew that sorcerers found the use of magic stressful and often tiring, which she usually took as a sign they were doing things forbidden to mortals. But this afternoon, the old woman had put body and soul into giving her that information. She needed to rest. Halina made sure the old woman was comfortable before she left, and put a twenty-guilder note on the desk, which she believed must amount to a day's takings.

It was worth every penny to know he would remain alive long enough for them to meet again.

***

The heavens opened as they left the Saunders' mansion, after the party thrown in aid of the workhouse. Indeed, as Kolinska had told Halina, Seymour seemed to have charmed Caroline into obedience, arranging all sorts of things for her to deal with her grief. It seemed a fitting end to an excruciating evening. Pan Wladyslaw Piech – Wladek to his friends and relations – felt humiliated, and part of it was his own wife's behaviour.

They sat in the carriage that was returning them to the hotel, Halina turned towards one window, Wladek towards the other. The roc feather on the crown of her enormous hat brushed his face, adding a comically unsavoury note to the miserable ride. Anger mixed with distress at being taken for a fool. He was not so poor at languages as they thought; to talk of a "Peak" within his earshot and expect him not to pick that one word out of their doggerel language as a name rather than a normal word was arrogance in the extreme. He believed they knew exactly who they had captive, and no doubt they were gloating over it. Halina had compounded it by asserting that it would be foolhardy to take the carriage to Lowe Road and invade the premises looking for his son. He could have got there and back before Seymour even realised where he was. His mind wandered. He had never seen Lowe Road and he saw himself running through the courtyard, through a dormitory full of bedraggled paupers, all skin and bone, to find someone who did not belong there. Could he really not have found his son amongst them? Was it really too dangerous?

With what Seymour could do with his magic, Halina had claimed, it was *easy* to imagine what contingency he had made for that scenario, including cold-blooded murder in front of people too intimidated to go to the militia.

But that his wife would not even let them try, nor confront the other two men and enlist their help in retrieving Michal. If they were blameless, then they would surely…

"Don't fret, Wladek," she said. "Your mind is polluting the air in here. Remember what Madame Kolinska said about the Angel. I think I know who he is. And Seymour has the devil's powers in him."

There was a time when she would not have graced that old witch with such a respectful honorific. She really had ensorcelled her, sapped her of her will to rescue her son.

"We're almost there," he grunted, noticing the lights from the hotel lanterns beginning to shine through the rainy night. They had stayed out here in Mereton, the least built-up of the southern districts of Ludlin, because Halina was afraid of going north of the river to the hotel in which Wladek had stayed in the summer. She had almost fainted at Pendlebury station when they arrived; it could have been put down to her having become accustomed to the wide open fields and forested hills and rivers of the Panczewo valley, but she had no problem with Galistow, where they had stayed the night between trains on the way south. "We'll be out in the fresh air soon – or what passes for it."

Their valet and lady's maid had been discharged for the night. Neither of the Piechowie wished to keep their servants standing up late to receive them when they came home late. For a grand couple with servants enough to populate a whole village, it came naturally to neither to mistreat them. In fact, Ela Spiller did meet her mistress at the door and accompanied them to their room, but Wladek had to make do without his valet. It demonstrated how frustrated he was when he made a cold remark to Spiller on the way upstairs that her loyalty was greater than his. It was Halina's turn to chide her husband for his poor temper when it had been he who had given Jendrek Kaczmarek the night off. Spiller admitted that she had found herself still up when her master and mistress were announced by the hotel butler, and felt guilty for simply leaving them to their own devices. Kaczmarek was fast asleep in their quarters, and no-one had troubled him.

As soon as they reached their suite, Wladek ripped off his clothes down to his shirtsleeves and then removed his trousers, revealing his long-johns. Halina was offended – he knew full well that he should not be so indecorous in front of a maidservant – but even so, she swallowed his effrontery with a glare and a sharp remark.

Spiller blushed and suggested her mistress go through to the other room in the suite, to give him some time alone. But Halina insisted that she wanted Wladek to calm down and forgive her. "The spirits are taking Michal away from us," she said. "Even you must understand there are some things that are bigger than we are."

"If I had my brother's regiment I would destroy that place," Wladek snarled, refusing his wife's imploring hand. "If I were twenty years younger…"

"But you're not. And you almost got killed when you tried to look for him. They caught you at gunpoint in Michal's empty house. If you died, or Michal died, we'd put the estate at risk."

"Like it's not at risk now!"

Spiller finally managed to take off the glorious lilac hat. Having been divested of it, Halina fell to her knees, asking his forgiveness.

"Don't be so melodramatic," Wladek said, sighing. "Get up."

It was a while before they got to bed. Halina disappeared into the bathroom, and washed. Wladek, used to his wife's vanity, patiently opened a book in the light from an electric lamp and listened to the rain drenching the city. She joined him, and extinguished the light immediately; he had to be quick to stash his book onto the bedside table, but he was used to this at home, and tonight was no different just because they were six hundred miles south of Dwor Kruczewski. Wladek huddled together with his wife.

"Do you know where he is?" he whispered. "I mean, can you *see* Lowe Road?"

"Yes," she said, with a sigh.

Wladek stopped and thought for a moment. In the coach she had not shed a single tear; the melodramatic behaviour was certainly unusual. He had been surprised at her desperation in the spring upon losing Michal, and was almost glad she had buttoned herself up again since then. Despite his frustration at her apparent lack of feeling, her anguish had unnerved him even more.

"I've wandered in my dreams to him," she went on. "I've reassured him on several occasions that I will look after him; he seems to be aware of me but I can't be sure. I don't understand why I'm not permitted to rescue him either."

"Where is he?"

"Now?"

"When you last saw him."

"In the servants' quarters," she said. "I projected in there last night. Seymour is using him as a personal attendant and a manservant for his niece. Once she leaves them he will go back to the general wards."

"So we couldn't get into the lodge to get him out without a struggle? Even if we went now?"

Halina squeezed his hand. "We'd come up across an insurmountable obstacle to any rescue," she said. "There's a... a *guard–dog* there, a large, grey presence haunting the site. I'm not too sure what it is, but as far as I can tell it is loyal to Seymour."

It sounded like a poor excuse. He really would get his younger brother down here with artillery and the elite Krovt palace guard that he commanded. But he didn't rouse himself, nor did he get dressed again, or fly to the station to return home to make plans. Zbigniew might have done so, but he was a muscular hussar, not a flabby, middle-aged squire. It was worth a thought, however.

He lay on his side, watching his wife fall asleep. Despite her distress, she was evidently tired enough. He himself found it difficult to simply slip into unconsciousness like that; he'd had many sleepless nights since the spring, and doubtless there would be many more to come.

If Michal came home to them, it would be by the gods' will. They both had to trust that the young man would find his way in the world and come back to them when the time was right.

STRANDS

Strands

Aisté looked around the tiny hut, angry tears collecting in her eyes. The structure was sound, but there was nowhere to sleep except the bare ground, grass still growing in the compacted earth. She gave her dirty hair a tired tug, removing the rag she'd used to tie it in a plait before they'd started on the long march from the railway-town. She'd slept with it like that for two days, too tired and depressed to comb it; some women had been able to keep their hair in good condition, others had just wound it up in makeshift turbans. Aisté had preferred to plait it back and leave it. Her town-clothes were filthy and worn out; they had been promised new clothing – probably accumulated from town rag-pickers and not brand-new off the peg of a department store – but for now they had to make do with what was in that one valise each they'd been allowed to bring.

Hers was just about exhausted of anything clean or warm. Her husband Skirman and son Gintaras hadn't been able to carry much in theirs, either; on the trains and in the way-stations they'd guarded everything jealously, afraid of their guards and even of the other deportees. She still had the cash she'd managed to collect up before leaving the house, but only because she'd hidden it in her underwear.

"Now you wish you'd gone with Algis," Skirman said from behind her.

"Would you have done anything differently?" Aisté asked, grabbing her dirty print frock in her hands to stop her giving her husband's chair a shove. "You refused to speak to Algis just like I did. Are you regretting not giving in to the promise of a traitor?"

"They consider us traitors, love."

Skirman seemed to be profligate with his fake wisdom. Of *course* the Empire considered them traitors. And one side had more power at its disposal to punish the false-hearted than the other.

It was a miracle they'd been able to keep his chair with them, and hadn't lost their cases in the general scrum on the march. There was some humanity left in the Empire after all. She supposed that they didn't want to kill them directly,preferring to grind them away into dust – specks of earth on the breeze, out of sight of the general rabble and therefore freer to dispose of them silently through cold and hunger rather than nooses and firing squads.

She yanked at her hair again, pulling it out of the plait which had stayed wound together after she removed the rag. Her cold fingers made it hard to tie a knot in the greasy fabric holding it in its ugly coiffure. A few tangled strands, the result of a month without being able to wash or comb her hair properly, came loose and she angrily threw them aside, wishing for inspiration. Skirman shuffled his chair closer, looking up at her imploringly, but saying nothing for the moment. "Don't look at me like that," she begged him. "Don't make it harder."

It was at least *summer*. By day it was already warmer than it would have been in Kubichas, but the afternoon was already cooling fast. The low sun shone directly in the hut door.

Gintaras came in, dragging the cases belonging to himself and his father. His face fell as he saw the inside of the shack. "When do they send us something to eat?"

"How should I know?" his father grunted. Despite the weather, he was wrapped in a tartan-print rug, bought in better days for picnics in the park.

Aisté saw them both look at her. She crouched down into a squat and retrieved the hair she'd thrown away. "I'm sure they'll bring us food at some point," she said. "They didn't neglect that the whole way here, and now we're settled, perhaps we'll be able to obtain better. I still have a bit of cash with me, and there was a signpost to a village a mile back up the road from the compound entrance." Which, itself, was a mile away at least, but thinking like that made it easier to imagine walking there.

"Do you think anyone will sell us *food?*" Skirman snapped. "Do you think they'll be *allowed* to?"

"They don't intend to starve us. If they wanted to kill us, they could just *shoot* us. It would be quicker for them, and they wouldn't spend so much time and money sending us here on the trains, or building us huts." She threw open their suitcases, one by one, and started clawing through them. Inside was mostly linen and wool underwear – petticoats, knickers, chemises, slips, stockings – and a couple of outer dresses, the plainest ones she could find. It might make the flock for inside a mattress if they were desperate. Gintaras and Skirman had more clothing in their trunks, but none of them had bargained on sleeping in huts on the bare ground. There was nothing edible; they'd had food with them at the beginning of the journey, but they couldn't have brought enough for the month-long journey that had been their fate. She was looking for something which would keep them from dying of exposure. At least Skirman had his rug – that was something. She'd brought her flannel nightdress and an extra layer was always a good thing.

It might be big enough for the two of them; they had shared it on the train while sitting up against the side of the carriage. Since he'd been shot in the leg a year before, by an overenthusiastic sniper on their own side who had misunderstood when the curfew began, he hadn't let go of it.

After unrolling every single garment in there and sighing in disgust at having brought nothing so useful as a quilt, her hand felt hair at the bottom of her own trunk. Curious, she dug out a mat – rather bigger than a doormat, but as thick and coarse as one. She didn't remember putting it in. There was a paper note pinned to it, which she tore off.

"*Mamma*," it read, "*I know you don't want to speak to me but where you're going, you'll need this.*

"*–Algis.*"

They'd been arguing as she packed. Him trying to convince her to stay with him and let him get them a free pass, since he'd been in the resistance and although they would have to leave Kubichas, they could go elsewhere as part of the general amnesty for...*traitors*. Her ordering him to pack a suitcase, and join them, the only honourable thing he could do after working against them in secret for most of the war.

His last gift, evidently made in secret and possibly by sorcerous means given how carefully she'd packed her linen, had been a *mat*. Of all the ridiculous things that he could have given them...Did he know they'd be left destitute in a mountain settlement? How had he got it in there? "Look at this," she laughed drily in the general direction of Skirman, who had taken the opportunity to nod off again. His injury had made him a complete invalid; he'd let go. They were all tired, but it was left up to her to sort their life out again. "Look at what *your son* gave us."

Skirman had dozed off while she hunted around. He woke up and gave it a passing glance. "Horsehair," he said. "My grandmother brought one of those over from the old country, but that's not hers – she gave it to my brother. It's a sleeping-mat. Quite appropriate for our little lodge here, seeing as how the peasants here weave them themselves."

"I know what it is," she lied, not wanting to give her husband the satisfaction of understanding something she didn't. "I wonder what mangy old nag gave itself for this." Despite her scorn, she spread it out on the floor, feeling what had to be tens of thousands of strands that had gone to make it and wondering if she herself could grow enough hair to make something this size for herself and Gintaras. She contemplated cutting off her unruly plait and weaving it there and then, but there were no scissors anywhere, and she'd need a lot more than what she had on her head.

"You take it, Skirman," she finally sighed.

"I have my rug," he said, looking up at her with understanding eyes.

"It's quite pretty the way it glints," Gintaras said.

She hadn't noticed underneath all that dye, but Aisté regarded it and noticed the sparkle. Tired and hungry, she *wasn't* in the mood to admire the thing as a work of art, although it undoubtedly was. It hadn't come from their house, so Algis must have bought it somewhere in the city, probably at a flea market for people bartering possessions for food or fuel at the end of the war. "I've heard they make it from Carriger hair," was her comment to her son. "That's why it sparkles. You saw the manes and tails yesterday," she said to her son, her hunger making her a little febrile, expending energy she couldn't afford to revel in the realisation. "You saw how mountain ponies look. They are said to be magically impervious to cold, and that's why they twinkle."

And then it hit her. She spread it out, hastily, still lightheaded with fatigue but now increasingly excited. It was gaudily dyed in native patterns, the solar wheels and the four- and eight-pointed stars common in northern Insulan and Littoral design. It could be Salvat, Krovot or Lenk, but they shared such patterns.

She sat down on it, knowing now why it might be a better gift than she had previously thought.

It didn't feel much different to an ordinary horse-hair mat. The strands crunched slightly under her bottom. She spread her hands out over the twisted hairs, fondling them eagerly, waiting for something to happen. Despite the dye, the sparkle was stronger, the colouring not hiding the hair's supernatural lustre. But whether or not it would work was the golden question. "I don't see how this works. It still feels cold." It had been enough, however, to give her some more hope. She looked at her husband with a frown. "It doesn't feel warmer than an ordinary rug – I mean, it's not heated or anything."

Her son came to join her, cuddling up to her. She put her arm around him; he too fiddled with the strands of hair in the mat, but if he felt something, he didn't say it out loud.

"It works if you believe it," Skirman said, knowingly. "I'll bet there's plenty of horsehair here for the taking to make new ones – you needn't claw your own off. My grandmother told me how she and her sisters used to go and glean wool from the hedgerows where the sheep had got snagged in the bushes, and sell it to the spinners. We'll have to live on our wits…"

"My grandparents had a slightly more orthodox view of faith. Trust in Lapiukas, but put on another shirt," she said abruptly, cutting him off. She realised her hand had gone to her pigtail and she was still picking lumps out of it.

"Try it out," Skirman said. "Lie down."

Cautiously, she did as he suggested, feeling the thousands of tiny strands against her cheek. Horsehair had gone into padding that she'd worn under her first stiffened skirt and into the upholstery of dining-room chairs, distant luxuries both. However, it actually felt softer and, now more importantly, *warmer* than she had felt it sitting up, as if she was lying on a living, breathing animal and cuddling it for warmth. A strand came away under her fingers, and she realised she was clawing at it. She shut her eyes, and the image of a pony flashed in front of her.

Every strand must contain a tiny snippet of the animal's soul, and the shaggy magic that kept it warm in the deep frost was now keeping her comfortable in the cool air of a mountain afternoon.

"Looks like it works," she said with a smile, still trying not to scrabble at the strands in her delirium.

THE ESCRITOIRE

The Escritoire

Andrew Russell took the key out of his pocket and dropped it onto the desk in front of Sister Alfrieda. "He got into my escritoire. I *cannot* have him rifling through my papers. If I have to resort to sorcery, then so be it."

"Your conscience troubles you for a good reason, Andrew," Alfrieda said, picking up the delicate item. "You believe you failed Robert Ashworth, but I think he needs the respite of an asylum rather than the rigours of a workhouse. It's a shame Simon seems so unconcerned with your privacy, but these things happen for a reason."

She held the key to the light. "Sorcery is not *forbidden* as such. It's a tool to be used wisely, and most of us avoid using it for frivolous purposes. But the blessing of a talent is meant to be used in service of the divine."

A flash of light ran down the key shaft, counter to the room's illumination. "Shall we test it?"

They left the convent and crossed the lane back to the workhouse. In the lodge, Russell's antique, lacquered writing desk sat in his bedroom. Alfrieda inserted the key in the lock and turned it. She felt the lock click, but when she tried to open the screen, it held fast. When Russell attempted to open it, it sprang open at a single push upwards.

He rolled the screen back down and locked it, afterwards holding the key lightly in his hand as if he wanted to drop it in the darkest corner of the room. Alfrieda suddenly felt her turban sag and had to rearrange it before it fell out of its elaborate folds. The silver filigree fastener at the back had come undone. Was this some sign that she should not have meddled in this affair? Had she been a Minervan nun caught casting a spell willfully rather than relying on the goddess' grace, she might be prosecuted by the church as a witch. However, the Frickan synod was more forgiving if magic was used, as she had said to Russell, in the interests of justice and peace. Fricka had not given her the ability to cast such small charms as this just to let it go to waste.

Russell lingered in the room. "Is there something the matter, madame?" he asked, a sheepish look in his eyes.

Before she could answer, a pink-and-grey blur stirred at the outer limits of her vision. "I fear you'll need a new clasp, Alfrieda" Simon Seymour said. "I just happen to have one that I was going to give to a lady friend, but I can always find her another gift. Oh, by the way, your desperation to keep me out of your private papers is understandable, Andrew, but there's no more need to protect Ashworth's particulars. He died today at Osbourne after the electric current they were using to treat him was applied too …enthusiastically. I'm so very sorry."

He handed over a small box in which there was a pretty clasp just the right size to pin through her headscarf. Before she could thank him, however, Seymour turned away, descending the stairs to his own apartments.

Russell dropped the key into his pocket. "He's wrong," he said without turning back to the nun. "There's always a need for the security of information belonging to the vulnerable. With that address I could at least have told his relatives of his whereabouts."

"Indeed. Let me make some more enquiries, Andrew. If Hedges' claim has any substance to it, then I'm sure someone can help me."

She opened out Seymour's brooch and replaced the old clip with it, which turned out to have broken. Almost immediately, the turban knitted itself tighter around her head – not tight enough to hurt, but tight enough that she understood who exactly was in charge.

Kupolinés

After the evening meal, backs began to straighten and eyes
brighten. A shower had crossed Carraig Dubh shortly
before supper, but the evening sky was now cloudless.
Giedré was up to her arms in water when Stanislovas came to her
and told her that the dishes could wait until the morning.

The "colonists" were being given back their shamans to go
with the priests that had accompanied them to the vast "compound"
in the Carriger mountains. The day before, a wagon had come from
the fortress, bringing him back from prison, an emaciated figure in
remnants of town clothes besieged by eager men and women
begging him for a charm against midges or a word from their dead
relatives. He'd been hustled away by soldiers before Stanislovas and
Eglé had got to him.

Those who had been older children and adults when they
had been deported talked all day in the fields and all night in their
cabins about finally being allowed to practise magic again without
the fear of being birched for it – or worse. The first solstice festival,
Kupolinés, permitted in ten years of exile had only been announced a
week ago, not time enough to organise anything large.

The glade where the festival was to take place was a mile
away. As dusk fell, the inhabitants of four villages were all on the
road together, dressed as much as they could in old town clothes or
motley made out of them. Children picked flowers from the roadside
and decorated their hair. Men and women whispered amorously to
each other. Giedré trotted alongside her adoptive parents, absorbing
their excitement without quite knowing what to expect.

There was a curious glow in the air as they approached the
priests' grove. Respectfully allowing the shaman his space, the
clergy they had been permitted to keep from their own indigenous
worship of Lapiukas stood to one side as the villagers entered the

space. Visiting priests of Lugh, the local Galtarai name for their mutual deity, stood by their side. Giedré resentfully eyed the soldiers feeding a massive bonfire; the shaman was meditating by it, his rags replaced with clean, new traditional dress and a fur hat styled to look like a fox, the image of their fox-god. Someone behind her muttered *"witch"* at him disparagingly, but most were smiling.

The moon rose over the mountain to the west. An owl hooted. As if on cue, the shaman stood, raising his arms to the sky. Stragglers still poured into the glade, but everyone fell silent. "protecting" the grove.

The oak tree around which the shaman had tied garlands of flowers erupted with the lights. At first, Giedré thought them merely the fireflies she'd seen on previous visits to the grove, but they twinkled with varying colours, which fireflies didn't do. With the clatter of wings, the lights took off into the inky sky, scattering to the four winds.

Murmurs started up. The question on everyone's lips was: *Are we freed?*

There was gunfire from the bushes in reply, the shaman falling forward into his own fire where he'd been shot in the back. Giedre panicked, and felt her body breaking in half, changing into her fox-form and rolling along the floor into a convenient hiding-place left by a rabbit. She emerged a few seconds later. All four of her paws took her scrambling into the bushes, as screams from human beings and the retorts from rifles filled the air.

It was morning when she finally stopped running, not sure where she was or where she was going, but knowing that her shapechange had allowed her to escape a massacre.

She didn't change back.

A NOTE ON MAGICAL CRIME

A Note on Magical Crime

(from the Brescester Gazette, *11 Harpa 1,985 IC)*

After recent events, it is evident that young gentlemen of fortune, living in Ludlin as the stewards of their parents' trade concerns, must take good care not to entangle themselves in any attempts on their lives and their property. The case of Alexei Volkovsky, son of Tirsk shipping magnates, and Vladimir Voronov, chairman of the Marcaster match factory owned by his parents' concern, is a particularly grievous "confidence trick".

The two young gentlemen were recently solicited by the philanthropist Simon Seymour, warden of the Lockley workhouse, to contribute towards repairs to the dormitory roofs at the similar Swellwater institution. The trouble began when both men arrived at the workhouse to discuss terms with the mistress there, Mrs Portia Wragg. Boris Silnov, formerly Volkovsky's valet and erstwhile secretary to Mr Seymour, invited them into a tavern opposite the workhouse, claiming Wragg was indisposed. Upon entering the "nip", the gentlemen were approached by Silnov's associate, Harold Frinton, posing as a country yeoman named Farrell, offering to buy the gentlemen drinks. Fortunately, Voronov spotted that Frinton had drugged the rum procured from the tap, alerted Alexei, and declined to drink his measure. The robbers then showed their true colours and tried to force it down their throats. The patrons of the bar intervened in the following brawl; both Frinton and Silnov were arrested and await trial.

Such attacks occur quite frequently to men and women both of property and of none, and this case would not be of note aside from two factors. Firstly, the wealth of the victims causes unease for many such individuals remaining in the city after the tragic disappearances of Michal Piech and Anselm Lederer, believed to be the victims of these or similar "skinners". Usually, the victims of such crimes are gulled, drugged or abducted and crudely stripped of their clothes and belongings. Their bodies are most often thrown into the river. Piech's house was looted and his valet Tarczowski kidnapped and murdered in a workhouse where he was being held captive by the mistress, the "Witch of Pendlebury" Aushra Vainyté.

Secondly, Frinton posed as Farrell presumably to evade identification if the crime was successful, as he was hitherto a respected Lockley courier with government patronage. However, this disguise was particularly notable because it was a magical mask, a physical changing of the features in the manner of the known sorcery allowing people to change into animals. Such powers pose a dire threat to the victims of crime. For good reason, witchcraft alone is no reason to prosecute a person. Frinton and Silnov went beyond the boundaries of lawfulness when they conspired to drug, rob and probably then kill their genteel victims by mundane means. However, the magical element of this crime stands out as worrying. Accordingly, attention must be turned by the Diet, Service and Provincial Cabinets to formulating a law against the practice of magic inimical to social relationships, lest the most heinous crimes should go unpunished.

Rasa

Arvid Chislenko cleaned his pince-nez and shook his head. "He's not going to survive. Let's move on."

There were now only a few new arrivals every day. A month ago, the elegantly vaulted receiving hall of the military hospital in Kubice had been full of bodies, and it had taken hours to determine who was treatable and who wasn't, most no longer being within the reach of help by the time they'd got to them. With the liberation of Rajnowka had come the biggest surge, but now the casualties dribbled in, fewer in number and mostly diseases from the surrounding countryside: the various kinds of waterplague and gaol-fever, or cholera, typhoid and typhus to give them their proper, scientific names.

At the moment, there were three patients needing attention, all delivered together, all wearing army uniforms with Krovot insignia.

"I feel a pulse," his nurse insisted. She was attending to the only blond among them, ignoring the others, including one who was a little livelier, and one who was completely still.

"Of course you do, but it's weak, no? It doesn't look as if he's going to make it. Let's take care of the one who's a little better."

The body of the young man to whom Rasa had chosen to minister lay on the stretcher, twitching slightly. Emaciated and exhausted, his hair was matted and dirty, and his lips cracked. Indeed, Chislenko could see them pulse and quiver slightly, gasping for air, but he could also hear the throat constrict in a death rattle as his body's functions seized up and shut down. Used to seeing the human organism as a machine, Chislenko knew this one was gasping and shuddering to a halt.

Rasa Maciulyté, on the other hand, obviously saw them as souls as only a village wisewoman could, and could barely let go of a single person until they really had ground their bodily gears into dust. He'd so far never been paired with her; she always went around on Motylecki's shift, but the sudden sickness of another nurse had forced him to work with her. "I think he can survive, comrade doctor. Hurry."

Chislenko took the "comrade" appellation with a twitch of his nose. He tried to find other ways of addressing people now. Despite having grown in sympathy towards the communists, these new terms stuck in his throat.

He picked up the man's wrist, intending to demonstrate that her method of triage was faulty. There was barely any pulse. The heart was too feeble to make much difference. "Indeed. But listen to his throat, Sister Maciulyté. Those are the last few breaths he'll ever take."

"Don't you think I know that? Back in the Cordon I heard it all the time."

Rasa was a thick-set woman, in the fullness of middle age, a peasant and most likely a sorcerer, a dabbler in witchcraft. Chislenko's assumption with most of the nurses was that prior to coming here, they had only received the most rudimentary medical training. It wouldn't be her fault, of course. The Lenks of Kubice and Syevirmetyevo had been deported wholesale south-east, to the opposite end of the Empire in Galtargh after the First War and put to work in the colonies of which she spoke "developing the wilderness". She might have been a young woman of twenty at the time of their expulsion, in the course of receiving some training at the hospital or in the art of a healer, but had her opportunities drastically reduced by deportation. Thousands had died in transit and in forced labour in penal settlements, but the survivors had gradually earned the right to a normal life, despite not being free to leave what was known as the Cordon until the end of the Empire ripped it down.

Meanwhile, every village, free and unfree, had its healer: its witch, shaman or druid depending on nationality. He wasn't prejudiced against them; they did essential work among people who had had very little access to scientific medicine under the Empire. There would still be the need for men and women with healing hands; Chislenko was sceptical as to how the new Commonwealth was going to establish a health system for everyone, and, despite its terrible unreliability, he knew full well magic made it easier to control the spread of disease under normal circumstances. As *lisitsocheskiy*, a worshipper of Lisitsok the Green, he even had no antipathy towards active sorcery like his Minervan compatriots.

But in a situation where they had to make snap decisions on whom to treat and whom to let slip into the Thrice Nine Kingdoms, this was holding up the good they could do for the other patients.

There wasn't much hope for this man and his comrades, found after an outbreak of cholera in a village just outside the city. Tomorrow and the next day there might be no-one here needing admission, maybe just a few drunks having fallen in the street and requiring a few stitches, or a woman begging for milk for children who may or may not exist. Unlike the disastrous way it had started, the communists had managed the aftermath of the war fairly well. However, war always pushed people into towns, which posed significant public health dangers. Fair enough; Chislenko was the first person to admit that after the First War, the military had abandoned the civilians of the liberated cities while privileging the soldiers and army workers, and for two years afterwards dispossessed peasants had died in the streets and workhouses of Syevirmetyevo from diseases caused by public health being simply overwhelmed. Laws had eventually been passed to forcibly return them to the countryside, but the most tenacious had held on to city residence as long as possible and built slums and shanty towns to prolong their lucrative relationship with urban life.

The communists strictly forbade him to turn anyone away without at least an audience from a nurse, whether they needed bandages or food. It was forbidden for him to take any payment for his work, even in kind, since he was completely provided for by the hospital authorities. Surprisingly, this had not caused a stampede of beggars flocking inside the compound, a mile from the city centre, and he had relaxed his opposition to it before they ushered him out at gunpoint and put a more pliant physician in his place.

Like the believing communist Motylecki, for instance, his former pupil but now his master.

He considered the situation of two of the other victims, and found someone worth saving. The other was dead, and Chislenko sent an orderly for a priest who could read the last rites over the body as dictated in scripture; the chaplains were over-worked, but they admitted that the spirit could be sent on its way after a body's death if there really was no ability to save someone. As he turned to the living man, the rattle of the man Rasa was attending to suddenly stopped. Chislenko dispatched the his patient with an orderly to the general sickness ward, and stepped back over to his stubborn assistant, expecting to have to order someone to wrap up two corpses.

The man with the blond hair mouthed his thanks and limply palmed the air. Rasa caught his wrist and gently put it down, back onto the stretcher. "No pawing. Save your energy," she commanded. "You're exhausted. You'll live, but you're terribly tired. Close those eyes of yours and we'll get you into a proper bed."

The patient groaned, a sigh that indicated his lungs were fully functional, and his body settled into its mechanical process again, lungs like the bellows of a factory furnace and heart like the ticking of a clock.

Nu bozhe Lisitsok, Chislenko scowled inwardly. *Lisak in Heaven. Why him? Why not the other two?*

"There you go," she said with an indulgent smile. "In a moment or two, comrade Doctor Chislenko will get someone to find you a bed."

"I'll do it myself."

Her reproachful gaze compelled him to start walking, but not so quickly as not to see what might happen next.

Maybe we got to that man first. Maybe it's not resurrection – maybe she's only able to revive someone from near death, and not bring someone back from Spirit. He'd heard of the latter ability in some very holy men and women, but never in his lifetime of hospitals and healers seen it happen. He'd seen people healed of the most debilitating and damaging conditions, heard of a man with scorched lungs from a house fire relieved and then cured, but he thought back. Once the death rattle had begun, the reasonable thing to do was allow the person to slip away.

As he himself put the healthier survivor to bed on the ward, his fingers pulsed for a few minutes, itching to get on with their business of repairing the machinery of life elsewhere in the hospital.

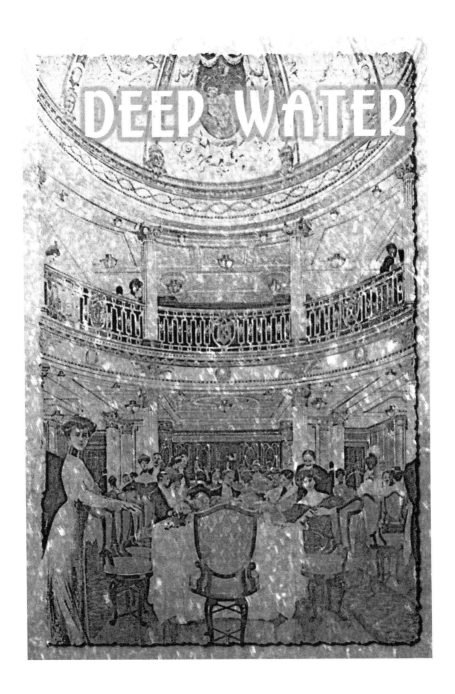

Deep Water

Ludlin was five days behind them, and Gansett three days ahead. The pitch and roll of the ship might have caused the odd napkin to fall from a lap or wine-bottle to slop a little more than was necessary into a glass, but they were nestled comfortably amongst the waves. Grigory Ivanovich Bykov could barely hear the ship's engines above the hubbub of the dining room, nor feel the gentle rocking of the waves as he trotted about the room shaking hands with the wide-eyed passengers, and that was the way it should be. The military governor of Lenkija preferred not to travel too far from land, but so long as aircraft could not cross water safely there was no other way of crossing the ocean to the Hinterwelt.

An assortment of notables from across the globe were mingling at the tables at which he briefly stopped to gossip and flirt. Later on some of them would be no doubt exchanging pleasantries in a more comfortable, horizontal position. Bykov knew of a few women who wouldn't mind his attentions, invited on board as second-class passengers to sample the elegance of a liner after the long Lenkish winter had seen them guests below stairs at his mansion in Saulepilis. All the same, he hoped to find an unattached young lady here in need of his intimate company, perhaps even of a good enough family to be his bride.

A waiter nodded his head before him and suggested he pour the governor another drink.

Bykov craned his head to one side, squinting, before deciding not to accept the offer. "What's your name?"

"Kah-Cheh-Ell 32592." He snapped to the same goggle-eyed attention as all the convict-labourers did.

"Don't give me that numbering bollocks. What's your *name*?"

The young man gulped. "Piasecki, sir. Marcin Piasecki. Are you sure I can't pour you anything?"

"Best not. Have you been in a fight, man? Your ear looks torn."

The craven man, probably not fully out of his twenties, went red. "It's a long story, sir."

"Can't talk now, but I can ask that you serve me later in my room and we'll discuss how you came by it." Bykov knew full well how someone's ear might be notched like that, and wondered why the man had been put up front and wasn't just stoking the furnaces below deck or hauling supplies aboard.

"If it pleases you, sir."

"Course it does, otherwise I wouldn't have asked." It was his job to find them something useful to do so that they didn't scrap in the hold, but this wasn't his first choice. At least Piasecki's corpse wouldn't dirty Algonese harbour waters. The time was at an end when this sort of thing was acceptable, and when they got most of them transferred to the Margins, they could just liberate the rest and have them colonise their own marginal land.

"I'll come and find you later." Bykov trotted away, scanning the room, while looking for a possible culprit — looking for someone he knew to be a magician. Piasecki's sponsor was taking a risk putting him where he could be interrogated rather than just having him act as a valet in their cabin.

Bah. Everyone's at it these days, he thought. *And some people have the ability to charm a whole room into not noticing they're using a convict-labourer to serve at dinner — and more.* Piasecki had come aboard in Saulepilis, but Lieutenant Elliott had reported him as delinquent twice and beaten him the second time, just after they transferred to the liner. He didn't do it himself; he let that odious Yuri administer it in secret. He would have been spotted later by the person who wanted him to wait at table amongst paid servants. Goodness knows what he was telling them in their mess.

He looked from eye to eye as he returned to the captain's table, the bottle of whisky half-empty and the dish of fruit reduced to peel, smidgens of pulp and seeds on the tablecloth. Bykov felt the ship give a half-hearted lurch, and he clutched his stomach. He hadn't seen anyone who looked like a sorcerer; he knew that the Algonese didn't frown on magic as much as the Insulans did, but all the same, suspicions arose because magic was so subtle and left few traces of its workings on others. When someone could read your thoughts, hide things from your mind, or spirit objects into strange places, it didn't do to let sorcerers slip past.

One magician could recognise another, and see what magic was being used to conceal.

He returned to his own table. Nootau Kigonz sat there talking to an Algonese entrepreneur. It was beyond civilised of him to accuse the captain of sorcery or harbouring a sorcerer on board. When Insula needed Algon's approval to move ahead with formal absorption of the two littoral states into the Empire, he could ill afford to upset any dignitary, however minor. The competing empires in the hinterworld laid claim to the northern icelands, and Lenkija's coastline met the floes head on, meaning its previous arguments with Algon now became Insula's. Maybe one of the Algonese ladies was using Piasecki as her exotic foreign gigolo; they were taking enough of a risk to go to any lengths possible to ensure she could make use of him and that he was kept respectable. The crew was mixed, and conditions were reputedly awful for any labourer in the bowels of the ship, which was probably why the waiters here were so obedient. One false move and they'd be knee-deep in coal and oil and the gods-only-knew what.

He poured himself another glass of spirits. Kigonz plucked the last plum from the bowl and ate it whole. Those of their status could bypass table manners whenever they felt like it. His straitlaced daughter, Chepi, regarded him with cold eyes and a toss of her head every time he or Bykov looked in her direction. Bykov understood from her topics of conversation that she was a shaman.

Strictly off-limits, Grisha, he instructed himself; *strictly off-limits. He wants to find her an Insulan husband, but I'm not that man. I don't think I'll ever be "that man", not after Vainyté.*

Just behind their table was a service trolley where a whole gaggle of footmen were clearing the slops. Bykov knew he should pay them no heed, just as they did not dare look over to their table to disturb their meal. However, Piasecki was there with them, fetching plates of leftovers from the tables abandoned by bored guests to scrape off the remains. On land, such detritus went to feed the pigs. His palace in the Lenkish capital had a whole sty of porkers who indulged themselves on the ruins of each meal. Bykov was minded to ask whether there were a few fat sows kept below stairs, or whether the convict-labourers took their place.

"So when do you hand over to the civilian authorities?" Kigonz asked.

"I hope never," Bykov said. "They've already postponed absorption another couple of years because of the restlessness on the mainland. If I had my way they'd never come out from under military rule, and we'd impose it on the rest of Insula. But Empress Sophia's covenant dies hard."

"And what of Vesgale?"

"The transition there is quicker," Bykov admitted. "We do have a definite date for giving them the full status of province. With Black Ieva captured and executed, bandit resistance fell away completely." He waved the whisky in the direction of the captain and his daughter. "The floggings go on in Lenkija until the population can be brought to heel."

Chepi shook her head at his offer, and Bykov pulled the bottle back. However, she changed her mind and picked up her glass and pass it to him. "From what I've heard the rest of Insula doesn't want to be an Empire anymore," she said, her eyes darting to her father's face momentarily. "With so many riots in your cities the army seems to be making things worse, not better."

"The army on Insula is restless because the civilian governors have tried to appease their rebellious populations too much," Bykov explained. "If it simply took over then the Empire could steady itself."

"Would you relinquish power at that point though, Governor?"

"That's enough, Chepi," her father said. "Don't insult our guest." The conversation on previous evenings had steered clear of politics, but tonight both Bykov and Kigonz had unbuttoned themselves.

The ship's movement through the water was smooth and graceful, but after the lurch which had almost deprived him of his dinner, the governor perceived a change in the rhythm of the waves. Piasecki came over and took up the empty fruit-bowl. "More would be nice," Bykov grunted. He shifted around in his seat as the ship's list got a little more pronounced. "Tell me: which master of ceremonies was it allowed you to serve here with your ear like that?"

Chepi blinked. "Grigory Ivanovich," she blurted out, "I took pity on the poor man earlier on. He was struggling with a bag of potatoes and almost spilled them — he appeared too weak to be doing heavy physical tasks. Surely the captain's daughter can have her moment of indulgence with such a fine fellow?" She smiled at Piasecki, who had the good manners not to reciprocate the grin.

"He'd be a fine fellow if he wasn't a criminal," Kigonz said. "Send him back to the hold; I'll get the taskmasters to see to him later."

Piasecki froze in place, unsure of what to do; Chepi stared down her nose at the table, her face flushing in embarrassment, seemingly unable to stick up for the man she'd played with on a whim. Bykov looked at the servant, then at the captain and his daughter, and shook his head. "There's no need to punish him for your daughter's indulgence. See that he's fed properly from the servants' hall and return him to the transport barracks with orders not to discipline him. I've seen what happens down there and I won't have it said that..."

There was a jolt and the ship's forward end plunged downwards, sending an explosion of white foam against the window. The dining hall lights jostled and flickered, but thankfully did not shatter and ignite any of the drapery. The guests gave gasps of distress.

Bykov and Kigonz both leapt to their feet and dashed to the portholes.

Thin Ice

The sky was darkening and clouding over rapidly. Olga Szumannowna could see flecks of snow in the wind for the first time that day. The ice was solid and the lying snow around the Adra thick and even, but falling flakes did not make for a comfortable skating experience. Her queue was only a few people deep as it is, the slate-grey clouds chasing the usual crowds away. There was no reason for the stewards to call people off the ice, but every reason for them not to pay her for the hire of skates.

She adjusted the shutters on the front of the kiosk to hog every last bit of shelter that she could. Her fur mantle and hood were adequate and this was her own business. With people still wanting to pay their two guilders, there was no need to pack up.

"An hour, please," the young woman at the head of the queue asked.

Olga regarded her through forensic, squinting eyes, taking in the red velvet pelisse, the high-crowned hat with a broad brim, the lace-and-fur hood inside it, and fronds of dark brown hair and white skin. She looked like the fairy-tale character Sniezynka — Snowmaiden — the girl who was carved from a block of ice for a barren couple to have as a daughter. Except Snezynka was pictured dressed in blue and white, like a frosty day with a clear sky, not blood red like the devil who loped across Salvatka in the old times, burning the peaceful wiedzmini and the oak groves, and subjecting them to eastern tyranny.

A gold pin in the shape of an owl glinted from the scarf draped around her shoulders. Olga snorted when she saw it and crossed herself with the points of the compass.

"An hour, if you please," the girl asked again, placing two brass coins down on the counter.

"It's unsafe," Olga snapped.

Her customer's eyes widened. "I've skated in this weather before," she protested.

Olga followed her dark gaze to a point behind her, and shifted to between the woman and where her eyes fell. "It's unsafe," she stressed again, and pushed away the money.

A few murmurs came from the patrons behind her, who turned to leave. "It ain't unsafe for yous lot," Olga growled. "Just for Bloodmaiden here and her cuckoo's eyes."

"I'm just as entitled as you are to skate here." The girl was old enough to be out on her own, but not old enough to know when she was beaten, or to respect her elders. She looked exceedingly well-off, too. Given that she was vostochni, Olga fancied she knew what family she was from, and she wasn't having them use her boots when they could well afford their own.

"Don't give me all that 'Imperial citizen' nonsense. This is a private establishment. I can serve whom I like, Empire or no Empire. He said so — you might have heard." Olga gestured towards where the woman had been looking a few moments ago. A piece of newsprint had been carefully cut out from Obrazki na Zywo, Living Pictures, the Salvat illustrated newspaper, and framed behind glass. It bore an engraving of Szymon Jaworski with a decorative wreath below the picture inscribed with the words Patriot, Liberator, Saviour. The whole icon had been strung with carved oak-leaf beads, an off-season substitute for fresh oak leaves.

She'd put it up there after the last pogrom to keep people who didn't fit in away. The young lady didn't need any more telling. She turned away, muttering to herself.

Olga turned back to her next customer, whose money she took without hesitation. The queue was two additional people shorter; they must have been cuckoos too, vostochni who also needed warning off. She supposed that if they had their own skates, they might have got past her, but that was their own business and that of the Tiergarten stewards, who did not attend to who was skating on their river. Affording most of her needs from her current business, skates in the winter, newspapers in spring and autumn and flowers in the summer, it did not hurt to turn them away at all. And none of the others were showing any solidarity with those she had rejected. She counted the wealthy among her patrons; she rented skates to people who made a spontaneous decision to go on the ice. But she could spot vostochni like a buzzard might spot a rabbit.

She heaved a pair of skates over the counter for the next person, and the next, and the next, before the weather descended in earnest and people returned to the kiosk to divest themselves of their rented blades or boots. She had a small changing room out in the back, where she could keep an eye on her customers; she was surprised that she didn't get more people thieving from her, but she did keep points of the compass above her door as a charm against that. That didn't stop the more willful, but it seemed to deter people from just not bothering to return them. She charged enough that she didn't get guttersnipes hanging about, or tempt women of relaxed morals into her room to solicit amongst her customers.

The rush started to die away, and she closed the kiosk. Before she left she'd have some of the chicken broth she'd brought with her. She could stay all night here if she needed to, bedding down on the benches in the changing rooms beneath the rows of skates.

As she finished closing the shutters, there was a piercing howl against the wind — what sounded like several frustrated screeches and then a scream. She shook her head and carried on with battening down the hatches and putting dried macaroni into the broth to boil. No sense in trying to find the origin of the noise — it was probably just a stray cat.

About an hour later, she finally left the hut as the wind died away. The snow was luminous against the dark, and the lights strung along the Tiergarten Embankment glittered in the fresh air. The clouds still covered the moon, but the oil-lights from tenement windows and the new electric lights from the street strung the night with "fairies and angels", as her mother, Lisak rest her soul, had said when she'd first visited the city.

She had to pick her way delicately along the shore. The park was low on the list of priorities at this hour. Workmen — prisoners and paupers mostly — would be clearing the tram lines and Targowa Street before they beat a path up to her shack on the beach. Stone steps led up from the riverbank to the cobbles and the enormous Targowski Viaduct across the river, large enough to carry two tramlines in each direction as well as an ordinary vehicular carriageway. The sheet of ice on the river was sound, she thought with a last, gimlet-eyed stare at it. There should be river ice for the next two months, then it would melt, and she'd have to get out the bales of papers that came in and take the skates to the lock-up. A few years more and she'd have to get in a helper to whom to hand the business over, hopefully keeping her discernment for respectable customers alive.

A patch of ice had come adrift at the edge of the river, about ten yards from the Targowski viaduct's pillars. She looked from side to side, wondering whether such a crack would cause the rest of the sheet to become dangerous and unstable. Skaters went on at their own risk, of course, but it was her concern that the ice remain visibly safe. A number of people died every year.

She looked up the steps to see whether anyone was about should she fall, and on the fifth stair she caught a glint of light flash off a metal object. Her boots were made to give her a good grip on snow, so she leapt up the steps and picked up the glinting item.

It was a tiny gold pin in the shape of an owl sat on a branch. Olga twitched as she thought she heard pleading squeals.

She looked back at the hole in the ice, which had begun to frost over again, and back to the pin. It was the same one that had been on the breast of the girl she had turned away from the kiosk.

You're not responsible for her welfare, she reminded herself. Bronislaw Komarczyk on the other bank isn't fussy. He serves vostochni like her; as likely as not he is one, but I shan't get involved. She might have gone to them.

There was a splash and a glug behind her. She turned round, but the icy water was still. Nevertheless, it had come from the hole. She clutched the item in her hand. A greater and more powerful vision of a woman — the young lady who had been at her kiosk earlier in the day — being pushed under the ice by invisible hands came to her, and she dropped the charm into her pocket in haste to get rid of the vision.

As far as she knew, Olga was not psychic; she had left all that to the wiedzmini, the cunning-folk witches in her village to the north of Achava, and to the parish priest Filomena Sajenczyk, a woman who had also been a great seer visited from miles around by peasants of both religious persuasions for her valuable counsel. Two or three others had passed on since her girlhood, but Baltazar Koszulicki was reputed to be following in Sajenczyk's footsteps as a promising holy man.

As she walked home, she also remembered a letter from her brother remarking that Koszulicki had been a jeweller's apprentice before he had taken holy orders. Albert Szumann had taken a necklace to him to appraise; he needed to raise capital to buy more bees for his growing honey enterprise. They could trust Koszulicki as a clergyman not to exploit his senses for material profit, and although he did not act as a pawnbroker himself, he knew who was reputable enough to give them fair prices. The charm looked old and rather valuable. If she couldn't save its owner, she might be able to see whether they could trace her family and return it.

If it held the resonance of the woman's last moments it might also be easy for a spiritualist to coax the spirits out of it — particularly if they themselves needed the help of the living to trace their killers.

After her curmudgeonly behaviour earlier on, she also knew she had quite a lot to make up to the spirit. But without having seen any of the incident in person, she couldn't go to the militia about it.

Acknowledgements

The Cat's Tail

Brian Holland - Corning, NY - Puddle Reflection
https://www.flickr.com/photos/bholl7510/14529556823/

The Doctrine of Impenetrability

Jinterwas - Sparkling Stars
https://www.flickr.com/photos/jinterwas/6510218257/

Birthdates

Duncan Johnston - Cosmo -
https://www.flickr.com/photos/duncanjohnston/6095683867/

Duncan Johnston - Second Life Beyond The Bokeh
https://www.flickr.com/photos/duncanjohnston/5369956773/

The Mesmerist

Renee - Photo Texture
https://www.flickr.com/photos/playingwithpsp/2949436311

Strands

Caleb Kimbrough - free_high_res_texture_449
https://www.flickr.com/photos/calebkimbrough/4991680463

A Piece of their Soul

Renee - OldPhoto
https://www.flickr.com/photos/playingwithpsp/3174806501/

Mogilyovka

Alice Popkorn - Magic Veil
https://www.flickr.com/photos/alicepopkorn/3402120831/

Where the Devil Says Goodnight

Renee - Torn
https://www.flickr.com/photos/playingwithpsp/3053304062/

fdecomite - Moon Halo - Lower Part
https://www.flickr.com/photos/fdecomite/348062829/

Kupolinés

Mary Vican - Sparkly Sunlight at the Beach
https://www.flickr.com/photos/26499572@N08/5028769858/

Previews

Brenda Starr - Texture 159
https://www.flickr.com/photos/brenda-starr/4694715707/

Rasa

Asja Boroš - Texture 122
https://www.flickr.com/photos/asjaboros/5319800318/

Jinterwas - Love Don't Live Here Any More -
https://www.flickr.com/photos/jinterwas/4548374825/

Jinterwas - Warm Desire
https://www.flickr.com/photos/jinterwas/4722197928/

Deep Water

Kevin Dooley - Wave energy - Fuji FinePix XP20
https://www.flickr.com/photos/pagedooley/7943901492/